Finding Mr Right

Welcome to the second book in Leigh Michaels's wonderful new trilogy—all about dating games and the single woman!

Meet Kit, Susannah and **Alison.** Three very special women who are friends, business partners—and happily single! Ambitious and successful, they live life to the fullest and have no room on their agenda for husband hunting!

But it seems they don't have to go looking for Mr Right…because each finds themselves unexpectedly pursued by their very own dream date….

Last month we saw Kit, sensitive and practical, organizing a bachelor auction and winning **The Billionaire Date** (March #3496).

Now meet Susannah—bubbly and impulsive, she thought she'd never see Marcus again after their affair ended. Until a work project brings them together and Susannah faces **The Playboy Assignment** (April #3500).

Next month, warmhearted Alison can no longer deny her craving for a baby when she meets a doctor who could help her, and finds herself taking on **The Husband Project** (May #3504).

You'll laugh, you'll cry, but you won't be able to put these books down as you share in a very special friendship between three wonderful women, and fall in love with the gorgeous men who—eventually—win them over!

Dear Reader,

Over the years, I've greatly enjoyed writing books which are connected—sequels, prequels and spin-offs. They usually come about because a secondary character in one book is so interesting that he or she demands a story of their own. But until now, I've never tackled an interconnected set of books, knowing from the very beginning that the stories would be so closely tied together that—while each book can stand alone—the three form a very special package. So the FINDING MR RIGHT trilogy has been both a challenge and a joy.

My editor and I had been talking about a trilogy for some time, and I'd been looking for the perfect setting in which my heroines could be business partners as well as friends. Then one of my friends mentioned that her sister was a partner in an all-woman public relations firm in Kansas City, Missouri. Now that was a story possibility made just for me, since I have a journalism background and public relations experience. And though, to this day, I know nothing more about that real-life PR firm than that it employs only women, I want to thank the members of that company for the inspiration they provided for the FINDING MR RIGHT trilogy.

And I thank you, my wonderful readers, for following along through the fifteen years since my first book was published, all the way to this new challenge. I think you'll enjoy meeting Kit, Susannah and Alison every bit as much as I enjoyed writing about them. I must warn you, though—I cried when I had to give up these three special new friends....

With love,

P.S. I love to hear from readers! You can write to me at:
P.O. Box 935, Ottumwa, Iowa, 52501-0935.

The Playboy Assignment

Leigh Michaels

Finding
Mr Right

Harlequin Books

TORONTO • NEW YORK • LONDON
AMSTERDAM • PARIS • SYDNEY • HAMBURG
STOCKHOLM • ATHENS • TOKYO • MILAN
MADRID • WARSAW • BUDAPEST • AUCKLAND

ISBN 0-373-03500-4

THE PLAYBOY ASSIGNMENT

First North American Publication 1998.

Copyright © 1998 by Leigh Michaels.

This edition published by arrangement with Harlequin Books S.A.

® and TM are trademarks of the publisher. Trademarks indicated with
® are registered in the United States Patent and Trademark Office, the
Canadian Trade Marks Office and in other countries.

Printed in U.S.A.

CHAPTER ONE

THE scent of freshly made coffee filled the small café, and Susannah paused in the doorway for a second to breathe her fill of the rich aroma. But one of her partners was already waiting in the back booth they reserved for their staff meeting every Monday morning, so Susannah strolled down the length of the long, narrow room and sat across from Alison.

She winced at the hardness of the green vinyl bench. "I'm either going to have to start carrying along a cushion or convince the management to redecorate."

Alison folded her newspaper and laid it aside. "The cushion would be easier. This place has looked the same as long as I can remember. So unless you're looking for a challenge—"

"Any reason I shouldn't be?" Susannah poured herself a cup of coffee from the carafe on the table.

"Only that redecorating isn't really a matter of public relations."

Susannah squirmed on the bench. "I don't know about that. My particular segment of the public would have a lot better relations with the management if—"

"*And* we've already got plenty of regular business to tend to. Which forces me to point out that you're late." Alison's tone was matter-of-fact, without a hint of reproach or irritation.

Susannah reached automatically for the pendant watch which dangled from a heavy gold chain around her neck. "Five minutes," she said. "And I'd have been smack on time if there hadn't been a bake sale going on outside the high school as I walked past."

Alison showed faint interest. "At this hour on a Monday morning?"

"Incredible, isn't it? I thought any teenager who was enterprising enough to be selling brownies this early deserved my support." She pulled a paper bag from her briefcase and waved it under Alison's nose. "So I bought both fudge and chocolate-chip cookies—but you can't have any till after breakfast."

The waitress set an omelette in front of Alison and grinned at Susannah. "What'll it be this morning, Sue?"

"Just a raspberry Danish. No hurry."

Alison picked up her fork. "Better make it bacon and eggs instead of more sugar, or you'll be bouncing off the walls by noon. Not that you don't most of the time, anyway."

"I didn't buy *that* much fudge." There was no defensiveness in Susannah's tone; Alison's comment was too near truth to allow room for resentment. Of the three partners in Tryad Public Relations, Alison was the practical manager, Kit was the steady get-it-done-whatever-it-takes sort, and Susannah was the visionary, never short of an idea.

The fact that nine out of ten of those ideas went nowhere had ceased to bother her—because the tenth was always a winner.

Of course, that had been true all her life. For every good plan she'd ever come up with, Susannah Miller had managed to find nine bad ones. Or sometimes, she thought dryly, an idea so far beyond bad that it was worth nine all by itself. That whole thing with Marc—

And that, Susannah told herself, was enough of that; Marc and the last of her disasters were eight long years in the past, and there was no point in rehashing the circumstances. The important thing was with two down-to-earth partners to keep her anchored to reality, her wilder ideas were squashed *before* they could get her into trouble.

Thinking of the partnership reminded her of the empty place where the third member of the triangle usually sat. "Tell me again when Kit's going to be back?"

"She said she was only taking two weeks off."

Susannah raised her eyebrows. "You sound a little doubtful. Have you ever known Kit not to keep her word?"

"She's never been on a honeymoon before."

"That's true." Susannah admired the smooth glazed surface of her raspberry Danish. She was just about to take her first bite when a photograph in the newspaper Alison had tossed aside caught her eye and made her forget everything else. "What's jolly old Cyrus doing in the press?" She put the Danish down and reached for the paper. "Pierce will be furious if he called in the media himself instead of letting the museum squeeze all the mileage we can out of the announcement..." Her voice trailed off as she saw the headline.

Cyrus Albrecht, industrialist, dies suddenly. The announcement was cool and dispassionate. Even the headline was in discreet black type, not the sort which blared from the page. If it hadn't been for the photograph—outdated by at least twenty years but still unmistakably Cyrus, with the beaklike nose and enormous ears which hadn't changed an iota with age—she'd have missed the story altogether.

"He can't die," Susannah said flatly.

Alison glanced at the page. "Well, I doubt the *Tribune* published his obituary as a practical joke. Why can't he die, anyway? At seventy-eight, I'd say the man has a right."

"Because he hasn't rewritten his damned will yet, that's why. At least, he hadn't the last time I talked to Pierce."

Alison nodded wisely. "I'd already gathered this is the millionaire art collector you've been dangling after for months."

"I wouldn't call it *dangling,* exactly," Susannah objected.

"The one who was so sensitive about causing speculation over his intentions that you couldn't even tell Kit and me exactly who he was."

"It's not that *I* didn't trust you," Susannah pointed out. "Pierce was afraid if there was talk—"

"—That the mysterious collector wouldn't donate his pretty pictures to Pierce's museum after all."

"They're not pretty pictures." Susannah saw the gleam of humor spring to life in Alison's dark eyes, and she wanted to bite off her tongue. "Wait a second. Let me rephrase that."

Alison was hooting with delight.

"Oh, all right," Susannah admitted. "Some of them—most of the modern art pieces, in fact—are about as far from pretty as it's possible to get. What I meant was they're more than just random paintings. It's a major collection, and it would mean the earth to the Dearborn Museum."

"Plus putting a finger in the eye of all the other places who'd like to have it?"

"Chicago's a big city," Susannah said stubbornly. "Why shouldn't it have another big art museum?" Her Danish had cooled, and the raspberry filling had congealed. She pushed the plate aside. "Of course, it's a moot point now, unless Cyrus signed a new will since I talked to Pierce. He might have had time, I suppose, but—"

Alison sighed. "All right, I know better than to think your mind will settle on the week's work schedule till after you've found out what's going on at your precious museum."

Susannah jumped up and gathered her purse and brief-case. "Ali, thanks a million. You really are the anchor that keeps Tryad from drifting off, you know."

"Cut out the poetic language and just go," Alison said tartly. "Before I change my mind."

Susannah grinned and flung an arm around Alison's shoulders for a quick hug.

Alison shrugged her off, but she was smiling. "Keep me posted, all right?"

Susannah feigned a look of shock. "But of course. After all, the Dearborn is Tryad's client—not just mine." She hurried out to the street before Alison could return an acid answer.

Morning rush hour in Chicago was no time to be hailing a cab, but today she was lucky. The taxi was going the wrong direction, but that was only a minor problem; the cabbie screeched to a halt in the traffic lane and Susannah darted across the street and flung herself into the back seat. "The Dearborn Museum," she gasped, "and hurry."

Horns honked behind them, and the cab screeched off, flinging Susannah against the seat.

"You want me to make an illegal U-turn, or can I take a minute to go around the block?" the cabbie asked dryly. "What's the rush, anyway? That place don't open till ten."

"I know."

The cabbie muttered, "People watch way too many movies these days, that's the trouble. Somebody's al-ways shouting 'Follow that car'—and thinking he's a comedian."

Susannah smothered a smile and refused to let herself be drawn into a discussion. Instead she stared out the window at Lake Michigan as the cab sped down Lakeshore Drive.

Despite the hour, several sailboats were already on the lake, their bright sails billowing in the early morning breeze. Far out on the horizon she saw a freighter, its progress so slow and stately that it was hard to tell if it was moving at all.

The cab turned toward downtown, and soon they were in the worst of the morning rush, fighting their way block by block between the skyscrapers, through the dark cold caverns where sunshine never fell. It was several weeks yet till summer would officially arrive, but some of these streets would still feel chilly in the middle of August.

Finally the cab swerved almost onto the sidewalk in front of the converted warehouse where the Dearborn Museum had found a home. At street level were retail shops; on the upper floors were small apartments, and the Dearborn was sandwiched in between. This year's goal would be to raise enough funds to improve access for the handicapped; Susannah's proposal for organizing the appeal was lying on her desk.

The Dearborn Museum, named for the frontier fort which occupied what later became the city of Chicago, had been one of Tryad's first clients. In fact, the tiny public relations firm and the struggling art museum had come to life at about the same time, both bravely taking on the challenge of competing with far larger and more established organizations.

Perhaps that similarity was the reason Susannah had so quickly taken the Dearborn to her heart. At any rate, Kit and Alison had been as delighted to leave the museum to her as Susannah was to take it on.

For three years now, she'd worked with the staff—which actually meant, of course, that she worked with Pierce Reynolds, the director. And she'd been as thrilled as anyone when Pierce had first made contact with Cyrus

Albrecht and learned that the old man was considering the future of the collection he'd so painstakingly built.

Susannah paid the cabbie and walked around the warehouse to the unmarked back entrance. She pressed the intercom button and gave her name, and a moment later a buzzer sounded and the lock released. She frowned a little as she climbed the narrow steps to the museum floor, wondering if Pierce had considered the need for additional security. Though the Dearborn's present collection wasn't shabby, it also wasn't the sort to draw the attention of thieves. But the Albrecht pieces would be different...if, of course, the Dearborn ever got them.

Pierce was in his office, a small, shabby, industrial-green room to one side of the stairwell, and the moment Susannah saw him she knew she didn't have to be the one to break the news. His blond hair, normally so neat it almost looked as if it had been painted on, was wildly disarranged. Even more unusual, his tie was at an angle, and the collar of his shirt curled up at the back.

"You look almost like one of your artist friends." She dropped into the rickety chair beside his desk. "The Bohemian kind who think that even *owning* a mirror is narcissistic."

Pierce's hand went automatically to his hair, even as he said, "That's not funny, Susannah."

"I know. I saw the newspaper." She hesitated. "It was a shock to you, too, obviously."

"Shock is hardly the word. Nuclear attack is more like it." Pierce sank into his chair and rubbed his temples.

Susannah's heart had dropped to her toes. "He hadn't finished the will?"

Pierce shook his head. "If I'd only pushed a little harder! He was talking about the details last week when

I saw him, and if I'd urged him to stop talking and get on with it—''

"If you'd pressed, he might have backed out altogether."

"I suppose so. But if I could have just made him see that the fine points could be adjusted anytime—''

Susannah had stopped listening. The fact that they had lost the collection was settling cold and hard in the pit of her stomach. Only now that the prize had been snatched away did she realize how much she had come to count on it. For months she'd been tentatively making her plans around the Albrecht collection. The announcement would be a boost to public recognition of the museum. The visitor list would increase dramatically, and fund-raising would be a snap.

Of course, she admitted, not all of her motives were so entirely selfless as those. The renown would make her job instantly easier. And part of the glory of the museum's success would reflect on Tryad, and therefore on Susannah...

She sighed. *Back to the drawing board,* she thought.

"It was odd," Pierce said. "The way Cyrus was behaving last week, I mean. I didn't realize it at the time, but—''

"Maybe he was already feeling ill?"

"No, that's not it at all. It was like he was teasing me, holding something back."

Possible, Susannah thought. And it was equally possible that Pierce's perceptions were being colored by twenty-twenty hindsight. "Cyrus was a world-class wheeler and dealer. Perhaps he wanted you to offer him something else, something extra, in return for the collection."

"Then why didn't he just ask? Anyway, what else could he have wanted?"

Susannah shrugged. "More power to influence the museum's future, perhaps."

"We'd already offered him a seat on the board."

"I know. Or maybe he was just playing out the game, for the fun of it and the attention it got him. He certainly liked having everybody dancing attendance on him."

"And he waited just a little too long to get down to business?" Suddenly Pierce's face brightened. "You don't suppose Cyrus made that will anyway, do you? Maybe he didn't tell me because he didn't want the attention to stop."

Susannah had her doubts, but this was the first positive note Pierce had expressed, and she thought it was hardly the time to discourage him. At any rate, before she'd gathered her thoughts, he'd picked up the telephone and was fumbling through his wallet. "Cyrus's attorney—what was his name? I've got his card in here somewhere..."

The business card he eventually produced had once been crisp and elegant, Susannah was certain. Now it was dog-eared, the edges frayed and the type rubbed and blurred—but not so damaged that Pierce couldn't read the phone number.

"I don't think he can tell you anything," she said as he dialed. "What a client puts in his will is a confidential matter."

"I'm not going to ask what's in the will, just whether Cyrus made any changes recently." He spoke into the phone. "Pierce Reynolds calling for Mr. Joseph Brewster, please."

The way Pierce's voice deepened whenever he wanted to impress someone had never failed to amuse Susannah, and even now a smile tugged at the corner of her mouth. She wondered if Pierce knew what he was doing. Probably not, she decided; the habit could well be so ingrained he was no longer aware of it.

As Pierce asked his question, he began to tap a pencil on his desk blotter at even intervals, and by the time he put the telephone down the steady rhythm had almost driven Susannah mad. She took one look at his glum face and forgot the tapping. "I told you he wouldn't answer the question."

"Oh, he answered." Pierce tossed the pencil aside. "Cyrus hasn't changed his will in years."

Susannah sighed. "I guess that's that."

"Unless he went to some other attorney, of course."

"Come on, Pierce—how likely is that? Maybe we should look on the positive side of this whole thing." Susannah tried to laugh, with little success. "With all those valuable paintings, and the publicity we expected to get, security would have become a massive problem. We'd have been begging for handouts in the street just to pay guards."

Pierce didn't hesitate. "We wouldn't have any trouble fund-raising for security."

Didn't the man have *any* sense of humor? "Okay, so it was a bad joke. But you may as well accept the facts."

"And if things had gone right we wouldn't have had to worry about securing this place at all."

Susannah frowned. "What does that mean?"

"I shouldn't have said anything." Pierce looked a bit shamefaced. "But—oh, what difference does it make now? I'd hoped that Cyrus would give his house to the museum, too."

Susannah had never seen Cyrus's home, but Pierce had told her about the huge old Queen Anne house, featuring all the grandeur of the high Victorian style, furnished with solid old walnut and located on a half-block square lot in one of Chicago's oldest and finest suburbs.

"And move the present collection there?" She shook her head. "It certainly makes our current troubles with access for the handicapped look like peanuts."

Pierce dismissed the problem with a wave of the hand. "Cyrus installed an elevator just last year."

Susannah rolled her eyes. At least, she thought, that harebrained scheme would never come to pass. Surely the board of directors would never have gone along with it...

On second thought, however, she realized that there was method in Pierce's madness. In fact, the idea made an odd sort of sense. In its downtown location, the Dearborn would always be just one among Chicago's several prominent art museums. But in the suburbs, it would stand alone, surrounded not by competition but by middle class families with time and money for cultural activities—not only visits but art classes, lectures, tours... Possibilities poured through her mind.

"Well, why not?" Pierce said defensively. "It's not as if Cyrus had a family to leave it to. Besides, his pictures were the most important thing in his life. Why not leave them in the setting he created for them?"

Reluctantly, she pushed the stream of ideas aside. It was too late for them. And too late, Susannah thought, for sympathy to do Pierce any good, either. She said, finally, "What about the funeral? Shall we go together?"

For a moment, she wasn't certain whether Pierce hadn't heard her or if he intended to refuse. Then he gave a harsh bark of laughter. "Oh, why not?" he said. "Doesn't every fisherman like to get a last glimpse of the one that got away?"

Susannah was on the telephone when Alison tapped gently at her office door and put her head in.

Susannah beckoned her in and said, "Yes, Mrs. Adams, I know exactly how disappointed you are. I've found, however—"

Alison sat down on the edge of a chintz-covered chair,

looking half afraid that the deep, soft cushions would drag her down like an undertow. Funny, Susannah thought, with half her mind still on Mrs. Adams, how different the partners were. Alison could sit like that, hands folded like a studious schoolgirl, for hours. Kit, if forced to wait, would probably have reorganized the bookshelves. Susannah would have flung herself on the overstuffed plaid couch and at least pretended to take a nap.

Finally she soothed Mrs. Adams into hanging up, and rubbed her ear as she put the telephone down. "Someday," she said, "I'm going to try to hang up the phone and discover that I can't because it's melted into my ear and become part of me." She looked longingly at the couch, but she knew better than to chance wrinkling her skirt. Linen—even black linen—showed every crease.

Alison smiled in sympathy. "Rita told me she'd put through calls from every single member of the Dearborn's board of directors today."

"Oh, she has. I can't decide whether to thank her for being such an efficient secretary, or yell at her—for exactly the same reason." Susannah's voice was dry. "Thank heaven that was the last of them—at least for this round."

"What's on their minds? Or did they all know about Cyrus?"

"No. Not by name, at least. But the news seems to have leaked just this morning that all hope of getting the collection has gone up in smoke, and every person who isn't running for cover is making threats instead."

Alison's eyebrows rose a fraction. "What kind of threats?"

"Oh, the usual noises about hiring a new director." Susannah waved a hand. "I think I got most of the feathers soothed. Eventually they'll realize it wasn't Pierce's fault—and also that they can't hire anyone else for what they're paying him—and everybody will be back on good terms. What's up, Ali?''

"Pierce, actually. Rita sent me up to tell you that he's waiting downstairs.''

Susannah stood up, smoothed her skirt, and slipped her black jacket on over her snowy white blouse. "Good. I mean, I'm not looking forward to Cyrus's funeral, but it's better than dealing with the phone." She picked up her wide-brimmed black hat and glanced in the mirror mounted on the back of her office door.

"I know. That's why Rita asked me to come up and tell you—because she didn't want to break into your call." Alison paused in the doorway. "You and Pierce look like a matched set, by the way, except you don't have a black tie and he wouldn't look nearly as good as you do in that hat."

Susannah paused as she adjusted the tilt of her hat. "You're sure it isn't just a little over the top? I don't want to look like a professional mourner. But I did like the old man, and as a mark of respect…"

"Looks great," Alison said. "If I could wear a hat with that kind of dash, I'd never take it off."

Susannah smiled in spite of herself. "They really get in the way when it comes to being kissed, you know."

"Just as I said—I'd never take it off." Alison grinned and started up the stairs toward the top floor production room.

"If you'd stop being quite so practical, Ali, you'd have lines of men wanting to kiss you."

Alison didn't even pause. "Really? Well, since I don't have time for that sort of nonsense, I'll *definitely* have to look for a hat."

Susannah made a face behind her partner's back and turned toward the staircase to the main floor.

Pierce was standing in the receptionist's office, hands clasped behind his back, shifting his weight from toes to heels and back again. He was staring at a framed poster which hung near Rita's desk, but Susannah doubted he'd even seen it, or heard her come in. She was wrong on both counts.

Pierce stepped back from the poster and said, "I could get you something really nice to hang there."

"On Tryad's decorating budget? I doubt it." She let her gaze run over him. In his dark suit he looked taller, but in fact his eyes were exactly on a level with Susannah's when, as now, she was wearing heels. His tie wasn't black, it was charcoal; Alison had been wrong. But she'd been correct about the rest. They couldn't have matched more perfectly if they'd been dressed by a single designer. Rita, she noticed, looked impressed.

Pierce had left his tiny sports car in front of Tryad's converted brownstone. He helped Susannah into the passenger seat, and she tried to keep her skirt from sliding impossibly high.

"At least it's a pretty day," she said as he got behind the wheel. "I wondered why the services were delayed so long, but it worked out beautifully, didn't it? After the rain yesterday and the day before—" Why was she babbling? The urge to talk simply to fill the silence was a sensation she'd never felt with Pierce before, and it took Susannah by surprise. Theirs had always been an easy and professional relationship.

"The funeral was put off for the heir's convenience."

Susannah frowned. "What heir?"

"Didn't I tell you what I've found out? The will currently in force was made more than ten years ago, and—"

Susannah interrupted with a long, low whistle. "You've put the delay to good use, haven't you?"

Pierce shrugged. "I don't know what use it is to know that Cyrus left everything he possessed to the son of an old flame."

"Well, well," Susannah drawled. "Who'd have thought it of Cyrus?"

"I know," Pierce said bitterly. "It's hard to believe that somebody as savvy as Cyrus was didn't bother to update his will now and then, even if his financial circumstances hadn't changed. A ten-year-old will is ridiculous...to say nothing of his leaving everything to somebody who wouldn't even bother to cut his Hawaiian vacation short so the funeral could be held on time."

"That wasn't quite what I meant," Susannah said. "It just occurred to me that perhaps the son of the old flame might be Cyrus's son, as well."

Pierce looked startled. "Oh, I don't think—"

"Even Cyrus was young once. And now that I think about it, there *was* a certain twinkle in his eyes sometimes."

Pierce snorted.

There were to be no church services, only a gathering in the cemetery. A surprising number of cars were already parked along the narrow, winding roads which cut the grand old cemetery into segments, and Pierce had to park at a distance. Susannah glanced from the gravel lane to her shoes, and sighed.

But before they'd gone far, the inconvenience of walking across grass and gravel in heels had given way to Susannah's love of old cemeteries. She'd almost forgotten how much she loved graveyards, full of elaborate monuments and family histories carved in stone in a kind of shorthand only the initiated could read. She'd been good at that, once, deducing from names and dates what had happened to the people who lay below the quiet sod. But she hadn't gone exploring for years now. Eight years, to be exact....

"But how do you know?"

The question echoed in her head, in an almost-plaintive baritone that she hadn't heard in the better part of a decade. Funny, she thought, that she could still hear it so clearly...

"How can you tell from a tombstone that life was rough for women?" Marc had asked on a crisp November day, as he stood beside her in an old cemetery in a far north suburb of Chicago. *"It's a man's tombstone, at that."*

"That's right," Susannah had said. *"The monument is for the patriarch, but look on the back at the list of names. His three wives didn't even get a stone to themselves. He married them one at a time, of course, but now they're all lying here beside him, together for eternity."*

"But how?" Marc had asked, very practically. *"He's only got two sides."*

Susannah had found the comment hysterically funny, and she'd finally wobbled over to a low flat stone nearby and sat down to recover from her fit of laughter. But in fact she'd never managed to get her breath back, for Marc had joined her there, and kissed her...

And she hadn't walked in a cemetery since.

"What a nuisance this is," Pierce said. "Trust Cyrus to make things inconvenient."

"Shush." They were getting close to the small tent where the crowd had gathered. A soft breeze tugged at Susannah's hat and ruffled the corners of the American flag covering the casket.

She hadn't known that Cyrus had been in the armed services. But then, Susannah thought, there seemed to be lots of things that they hadn't known about Cyrus.

They were almost the last to arrive, and only a few moments later a man in flowing robes began the service. Susannah tipped her head a little, allowing the wide brim of her hat to shield her eyes as she glanced around the crowd.

She saw a few vaguely familiar faces, but no one she

knew well. And try as she might, she couldn't locate any likely candidate to be—what was it Pierce had called him? The son of the old flame, that was it. No one stood out from the crowd. There was no row of chairs, no one obviously fighting strong emotion...

Perhaps, she thought, Pierce was wrong and the heir hadn't showed up after all?

The service was brief. From a distant hillside, a rifle salute cracked the air, taps sounded, and an honor guard briskly and efficiently folded the flag which had covered Cyrus's mahogany casket.

Susannah watched with interest as they presented it to a man standing nearby. But all she could see was the back of a well-groomed head and a brilliant white shirt collar showing between sleek black hair and a gray pin-striped suit. Not black, she thought, with interest.

"That must be the old flame's son," Pierce muttered into her ear. "Wish I could get a better look."

The pastor said a final prayer, then looked out over the crowd, drawing them all together with his gaze, and said, "It was Cyrus's request that everyone who attended this service be invited back to his home immediately afterward, for a party."

Susannah smothered a gasp. "That's macabre!" she whispered.

"What it is," Pierce muttered, "is a waste of money the museum could have put to far better use. A party! What nonsense."

But instead of turning back toward the city, Pierce followed the trail of cars toward the western suburb where Cyrus had lived.

"Wait a minute," Susannah said. "Surely you don't intend to go to the party, Pierce. Both of us think it's bad taste—"

"That's beside the point," Pierce said grimly. "Odds

are the old flame's son has equally bad taste, or he wouldn't have gone along with the idea."

Susannah thought about that sleek dark head, and frowned. "I don't quite see—"

"He probably doesn't have a clue about what to do with Cyrus's old pictures. Maybe he doesn't even realize that they're important. So maybe I can introduce myself and make another stab at the collection."

"Pierce, isn't it time to give up?"

"What kind of PR person are you, anyway? We can't lose by just asking. You'd feel like an idiot if he gave it to somebody else—or threw it away—because we didn't tell him we're interested."

He was right. In any case, she was going to end up at the party, since throwing herself out of a moving car didn't strike Susannah as much of an option. So she might as well give the idea a stab.

Cyrus Albrecht's house wasn't just a Queen Anne, she realized as Pierce pushed open the wrought-iron gate to the front walk. It was the most elaborate Queen Anne she'd ever seen. Towers and porches and balconies sprouted from everywhere she looked. The details of gingerbread and moldings and finials had been picked out in a palette of soft greens and browns, with an occasional startling touch of red.

"It would make a great haunted house," she said. "All it needs is a full moon and a few spider webs. But I don't see it as a full-fledged art museum—there can't be enough big walls."

Pierce shrugged. "We could have built a new wing. But that's out of the question now. This house is worth a fortune, the heir wouldn't even consider donating it."

Susannah paused. "The paintings are worth a fortune, too."

"But everybody has an idea what a house like this

will sell for. On the other hand, to an inexperienced eye, the paintings might not look like much at all.''

"Pierce, you *can't* misrepresent—''

They reached the front door, standing open to the summer breeze, and the murmur of the crowd reached out to them. Susannah knew her protest would carry back inside, so she bit her tongue and resolved to have it out with Pierce later.

They stepped across the threshold into the enormous dark-paneled front hall. Despite Susannah's hat, the change from sunlight to dimness blinded her for an instant. Before she saw the heir, who stood with his back almost squarely to the door, Pierce had already moved toward him, pulling her along. His right hand went out, demanding the heir's attention, and in the deepest voice she'd ever heard Pierce use, he said, "I'm sorry we meet on such a sad day. I was a friend of your.... I mean, of Cyrus's. I have a bit of an interest in art, too, you see.''

Susannah stared up at him in shock. *A bit of an interest?*

"Indeed," the heir said, and his voice echoed through Susannah's brain like the boom of a cannon.

Like a wooden marionette who could move only one joint at a time, she turned away from Pierce toward the heir. Under the wide brim of her hat, she spotted the monogram on his shirt cuff as he reached out to shake Pierce's hand. MDH, it said, in delicate embroidery.

MDH... Marcus David Herrington.

Marc, who had been the single biggest mistake Susannah Miller had ever made. Marc, who had prompted the most disastrous idea of a long and varied series.

Marc...

Slowly, afraid of what she would see, she lifted her eyes to his.

CHAPTER TWO

EVEN as she raised her head to look at him, Susannah told herself it was impossible. The Marc Herrington she'd known hadn't even owned a necktie, much less a pin-striped suit, and he was far more likely to flash a rude slogan on the front of a sweatshirt than his initials embroidered on a cuff.

Impossible.

She'd set herself up, that was what had happened. The walk through the cemetery had prompted her to think of Marc—and once those memories had been activated, all it took to set them spinning out of control again was a baritone voice and a chance monogram....

It *was* quite a coincidence, those initials. But the voice was easily explained; this man did sound a little like Marc—or, to be more accurate, her eight-years-old memory of Marc.

Susannah fixed a smile on her lips so she could properly greet a man who was not—who could not be—Marcus Herrington.

And she looked up into a pair of wide-set brown eyes, surrounded with a forest of long, dark, curly lashes. Eyes she had thought, once or twice, that she could drown in. Including that day eight years ago in the cemetery, when he had kissed her so long and so well that her scattered senses had allowed the worst idea of her life to look like a winner.

Marc's eyes. It was impossible—but it was also undeniable.

"Well," he said. In his rich baritone, the single word seemed to carry an entire encyclopedia of meaning. Or

24

did it only seem that way to Susannah's guilty conscience?

Not guilty, she reminded herself. She'd been foolish, yes—and impetuous and perhaps even idiotic—but she had nothing to feel guilty about.

She held out her hand to him and willed her voice to stay steady. "Marc."

His hand was warm and firm and strong. Susannah's fingers felt fragile and shaky in his grip.

Pierce stared down at her. Though he was obviously thunderstruck, he recovered in moments. "You know each other? But—but that's wonderful! Old friends, I suppose?"

Prompted, Susannah stumbled through the introductions.

"Marcus Herrington," Pierce said thoughtfully. "I don't believe I've heard the name."

"Oh, of course Susannah wouldn't have mentioned *me*," Marc said. Only the slightest emphasis set the last word apart, but there was no more doubt in his voice than there was humor in his smile.

Irritation surged through Susannah's veins. His meaning could hardly have been clearer even if he'd come straight out and said they'd been lovers. Of course, if he had, she could not only have denied it, but any listener would have doubted his motives. This was far more cunning. The implication was perfectly obvious—she could see from the expression in Pierce's eyes that he'd gotten the message loud and clear. And yet Marc hadn't really said a thing.

"No, I don't believe I ever brought up your name," she said coolly. "You were hardly important enough."

Marc lifted his eyebrows. "But of course, my dear. What else could I possibly have meant?"

That you were too important to talk about. Which was precisely what Pierce was thinking right now.

Susannah's annoyance was mixed with reluctant admiration at the way he'd so neatly boxed her into a corner. The Marc she'd known had been as transparent as glass. Just when—and how—had the man learned to be so smooth?

Not that it mattered, Susannah told herself firmly, what Pierce—or anyone else—thought.

Marc had turned back to Pierce. "It's rude of me to bring up ancient history. You shared Cyrus's interest in art, you said?"

The tinge of irony in Marc's voice was so subtle that Susannah almost doubted her own ears, despite the demonstration she'd just suffered at his hands. For an instant she wondered if he'd recognized Pierce's name, and therefore doubted the casualness of his interest. But she concluded that wasn't likely; the Dearborn was far from prominent as yet, and its director was hardly a household word across the country.

Then she followed Marc's gaze over Pierce's shoulder to one of Cyrus's favorite and most recent acquisitions, and knew why he was feeling ironic.

"I find his taste—shall we say, interesting?" Marc went on. "Personally, I'd probably use that thing to wipe the mud off my shoes."

Susannah braced herself.

The work was a long way from being her favorite. The artist—and she used the term loosely where Evans Jackson was concerned—had used a housepainter's brush to smear three slashes of blood-red pigment on a huge white canvas, and then left it to drip. Susannah thought it looked like something from a butcher's shop.

Pierce, on the other hand, considered the painting a master work. When he'd taken Susannah to the gallery to see Cyrus's new purchase, Pierce had been shocked by her lukewarm reaction. He'd spent the next half hour instructing her on artistic genius and the intricacies of expressionistic symbolism—at least Susannah thought that was what he'd called it. Her eyes had begun to glaze only a couple of minutes into the lecture.

She couldn't wait to see Marc's reaction to that same speech.

Pierce, too, had turned to look at the painting. "Oh, well, that sort of thing," he said tolerantly. "Cyrus would have his little jokes now and then."

Susannah blinked in surprise, remembering the outlandish price he'd told her Cyrus had paid. Then the metallic taste of fear rose in her throat. She'd forgotten, for just a moment, Pierce's implication that he only dabbled in art. Surely, she thought, he wasn't crazy enough to continue that charade, now that he'd had a chance to take Marc's measure...

"Not all the collection is so blatant," Pierce went on. "Cyrus actually had a few pieces which aren't half bad."

A voice in the back of her brain told her to stop him, no matter what it took, before he offered to do Marc a favor by taking the problematic pieces off his hands. But she was mesmerized by the pressure of Pierce's fingers on her elbow, and unable to protest.

"Blatant," Marc murmured. "What an interesting choice of words."

"In fact," Pierce went on, "if you're looking for someone to help value things for the estate—"

"That's very thoughtful," Marc said. "I wonder where Joe Brewster went. He's the one who'll handle all that." He glanced around the foyer, his six extra inches of height giving him the advantage of being able to look over most of the crowd, and gestured to someone Susannah couldn't see.

Joe Brewster. The name hit her like a rock. Brewster was Cyrus's attorney—the one Pierce had talked to about the will. If Joe Brewster recognized Pierce's name...

Pierce, however, seemed unconcerned. His smile was firmly in place.

A short, round man hurried up. "You wanted me, Marcus?"

"Joe, I'd like you to meet Susannah..." Marc paused. *Doesn't he even remember my name?* Susannah thought irritably. "Miller," she said coolly.

"Still? Or again?"

Susannah felt marginally better. Marc's hesitation made sense after all; there *was* a good chance that in eight years she'd have married—and perhaps divorced, as well. At least he hadn't assumed she'd married Pierce; maybe she should award him a point or two for that. "Still."

"What a shame," Marc said softly. "I seem to re-member you were determined to have a wedding. And with good reason, too."

Fury rose in Susannah's throat. *And if he solicitously asks what went wrong with my plans,* she thought grimly, *I'll strangle him!*

But Marc had moved straight on to introduce Pierce. "He's offered to help appraise Cyrus's collection, Joe."

The attorney stretched out a hand. "That's very gen-erous of you, Mr. Reynolds. Your opinion would be val-uable. As the director of the Dearborn—"

Pierce's fingers tightened on Susannah's elbow; it was the only sign of surprise she could detect. "Actually," he said casually, "I didn't exactly volunteer my services. The time constraints which come along with my job pre-vent me from doing appraisals. What I meant to say was, if you'd like help valuing the estate's art, I'm sure Susannah would be happy to pitch in."

Susannah opened her mouth to protest, and closed it again. She felt like a balloon with a slow leak. Now she knew that tightened grip of Pierce's hand hadn't been due to surprise after all; it had been more in the nature of a warning. He'd had this planned all along.

She could feel Marc's gaze drifting over her face, appraising every feature, every expression. "And Susannah is...qualified?" he asked.

She couldn't stay silent any longer. "Pierce, I hardly think that I—"

"Nonsense," Pierce said firmly. "Of course she's qualified. Don't underestimate your talent, Susannah."

"Or your resources," Marc added, very gently. "You know, Joe, I believe I just might take more of an interest in Cyrus's collection myself—under the circumstances."

His hand still on her elbow, Pierce guided Susannah across the foyer and into the broad hallway that led toward the dining room at the back of the house. Most of the crowd had moved on toward the buffet tables, and for a few moments, in the shadow of the staircase, the two of them were completely alone.

"I think that went very well," Pierce said.

The note of self-satisfaction in his voice grated on Susannah's nerves. "Then all I can say is that I'd like to see your definition of a disaster. The only thing that could have made it worse was if you'd offered to buy everything outright at some bargain-basement price."

Pierce tipped his head to one side and considered. "It's an idea. Herrington might actually have gone for it."

Susannah went on ruthlessly. "But Mr. Brewster would know you were trying to scam his client, and then you'd be in the soup and the museum would lose all credibility."

"That's an interesting point," Pierce mused. "Why he knew me, I mean—I didn't mention the museum when I called about the will. Cyrus must have told him about me along the way. Susannah, do you really believe I'm so shortsighted I'd try to pass myself off as an amateur?''

"It looked to me as if you were making a pretty good stab at it.''

"I did nothing of the sort. I simply didn't boast of my position, my education, or my background. If the man wanted to draw conclusions—''

Susannah stood her ground. "You deliberately tried to convince him that the Evans Jackson canvas is worthless.''

"I was being diplomatic. Feeling out his tastes. Trying to establish a bond. All good gallery owners do that sort of thing, or they'd never sell a single piece. It's no thanks to you, by the way, that I read him so clearly. Why didn't you tell me you knew him?''

"Because I didn't know it myself till it was too late to run," Susannah admitted.

"You did look a little stunned," Pierce admitted. "What was all that stuff about weddings, anyway? You didn't *marry* the man, did you?''

"No." Susannah's throat was dry, her voice taut.

"That's good. If you had, I'd really wonder about your judgment. I grant you, for a couple of minutes I was a bit unsure about him, myself. His clothes weren't bad, not bad at all. And the name... I wonder how somebody like that ended up with such an aristocratic name.''

"Funny," Susannah muttered. "My mother asked almost the same thing once.''

"But I knew as soon as he looked blankly at that magnificent Evans Jackson canvas that my first instinct was right." Pierce shuddered. "The very idea of threatening to wipe his feet on it! I only hope Evans doesn't hear what *I* said about his work.''

"I doubt the two of them hang around in the same circles.''

Pierce laughed. "That's certainly true."

"And all good gallery owners talk that way, don't they, to gain the customer's confidence?" Susannah didn't even try to keep the sarcasm out of her voice. "Pierce, about this assignment you've saddled me with... Surely you don't expect me to pass myself off as a staff member, because I won't do it."

"Oh, no. We'll refer to you as—let's see..."

She cut in ruthlessly. "We'll call me exactly what I am—the museum's public relations representative."

"Actually," Pierce mused, "that's ideal. Because of your inexperience—"

"I thought you told Marc I was qualified."

Pierce shrugged. "I didn't say expert. So any errors can easily be passed off—"

"Are you saying you want me to make errors?"

"Susannah, my dear, you'll have all of the museum's resources to draw on. And I expect you to use all the expertise the Dearborn can provide. Including me."

"I suppose that means *you'll* make the errors? Never mind."

"I'm still determined to end up with this collection, Susannah. So just remember—if you value things high, you'll have to raise the money to pay for them and explain to the board why they're worth so much."

"And if I value them low, I'll end up looking like a fool."

"Oh, I doubt that," Pierce said easily. "Didn't you see the way he was looking at you—sort of like a hungry wolf? I imagine, if you play your cards right, you'll be able to keep Marcus Herrington from asking any questions at all."

Tryad's office, a converted brownstone not far from the green expanse of Lincoln Park, was quiet when Pierce dropped Susannah off early that evening. The same couldn't be said of the rest of the neighborhood; since it was still mostly residential, the streets really came alive after work and school were over. And with the newly warmer weather to celebrate, kids were out in force.

Susannah dodged two roller skaters, paused to observe a cutthroat marbles tournament, finished teaching the two little girls next door a rope-skipping rhyme from her childhood, and stopped to study a hopscotch layout drawn in chalk on Tryad's own front walk.

"You know," she told the hopscotch artists, "this doesn't make us look very professional, having big white-numbered squares drawn on the concrete leading straight to our offices."

The girls looked stricken. "But we drew it as neatly as we could, Susannah," one of them said.

Another chimed in, "And it's only chalk, you know. It'll wash off when it rains."

The third added, "Maybe we could use colored chalk next time. It'd be prettier. Would that help?"

Susannah laughed, shook her head, and skirted the carefully drawn hopscotch field. The hopscotch craze would last only a few weeks; good neighbors—of any age—went on forever.

Almost automatically, she waved at the bay window of the house on the other side, the twin half of Tryad's brownstone. She wasn't surprised to see the white lace curtain flutter as if the corner had been hastily dropped. Mrs. Holcomb might be a recluse, but there wasn't a move made in the neighborhood which escaped her.

What did startle Susannah was a glimpse of a hand behind the curtain, half raised in what might have been a hesitant wave. It was the first time Mrs. Holcomb had ever responded directly to any approach Susannah had made, and she was surprised at the surge of pleasure which swept over her.

Such a little thing a wave was, to cause such a reaction. And yet, for Mrs. Holcomb—who, so far as Susannah knew, had left her house only once in the three years since Tryad had moved in next door—it was a major overture of friendship.

Inside, the office was dim and quiet. A few rays of late sunshine found their way in through the stained-glass panel at the top of the main stairway, and security lights glowed here and there, lighting the way to the exits. The usual hum of copy machines and computers, and the muted chime of the telephones, had stilled into silence.

In the receptionist's office, once the brownstone's living room, Rita's desk was neat, the blotter empty except for tomorrow's to-do list. The in-basket marked with Susannah's name was empty.

That was one minor miracle, Susannah thought. At least she was no farther behind than she'd been early this afternoon—it felt like a million years ago—when she'd left the office to attend Cyrus's funeral...

Except, of course, for the job Pierce had dumped on her. Putting a value on an art collection was hardly a public relations job, but Susannah liked both art and research, and under other circumstances she might have found it an enjoyable challenge. If she had plenty of time, if she didn't have a dozen pressing projects...

"Be honest," she told herself. "If it didn't involve Marc Herrington, you'd like the job a whole lot better."

She climbed the stairs from the main level to her own office, at the back of the building. Her desk was in chaos, piled with papers and folders, just as it had been late this morning when the telephone calls started to come in. The project she'd been working on was due to be presented to the client tomorrow afternoon, but Susannah had no enthusiasm for facing the final details tonight. She'd come in early in the morning to finish.

She sailed her picture hat across the room toward the chintz-covered couch. The hat landed almost atop a calico cat, curled up nearly out of sight under the edge of a cushion. The cat opened one yellow eye and surveyed her warily. Susannah apologized and went on down the hall to Kit's office, with its view of the street and the green expanse of Lincoln Park beyond.

The room was unnaturally neat, and Susannah thought the air smelled a bit stale after ten days of disuse. She wasn't quite sure how that could happen, since the door had been open all the time. Perhaps it wasn't staleness she felt, but loneliness.

She flung herself down on the chaise longue. She missed Kit. Missed being able to bounce ideas off her, to share frustrations and problems and triumphs.

"So what would Kitty do?" Her voice was loud in the silence of the office.

Stupid question, of course. Susannah would have bet money that Kit—straightforward, uncomplicated Kit—had never had a secret in her life. She'd even fallen in love so transparently that Susannah and Alison had known it almost before Kit herself had.

Susannah sighed.

Alison, the warmhearted and practical, wouldn't be much more help. She'd be sympathetic, of course, but Alison—who had X-ray vision when it came to predicting the outcome of a business decision—would never comprehend how, even at the tender and inexperienced age of eighteen, Susannah could have been so foolish, so impractical, so shortsighted.

The truth was, if she tried for a month Susannah couldn't explain to Alison what had happened eight years ago between her and Marc—because she wasn't certain she understood it herself.

And neither Kit nor Alison would be able to fathom why they'd never heard about Marc Herrington before.

If he had once been an important part of Susannah's life, they should have known all the details long since. And if he hadn't been significant, why was she making such a fuss about meeting him again now?

No, Susannah decided, her partners would be no help whatsoever. She was in this one on her own.

The last rays of sunlight were still filtering through the hallway, but Kit's office had dimmed slowly and imperceptibly till Susannah was sitting in darkness.

Maybe she was overreacting, she told herself hopefully. Despite what Marc had said about being involved in the fate of Cyrus's art collection, perhaps he really had no intention of doing anything of the sort. Maybe he'd just been pushing buttons, simply to see what her reaction would be. She wouldn't put that sort of behavior past the new Marc.

Besides, the collection was big, and with her lack of experience, valuing it wouldn't be the work of a few days. The task could stretch over a period of months, especially since she couldn't just drop her other obligations. Surely Marc couldn't rearrange his life to leave room for that.

Marc wasn't the sort to be without a job. He'd never been too proud to work at whatever came to hand, and Susannah doubted that had changed. Besides, hadn't Pierce said something about Cyrus's funeral being delayed because Marc was on vacation? A vacation surely implied a job, and also an employer—who would not be likely to look kindly on a lengthy absence.

But what kind of a job? she found herself wondering.

Once, Marc had been a welder in a factory which built farm machinery. She supposed he might have made the jump into management, pushing numbers instead of steel. As a supervisor of sorts, perhaps; his hands— though not calloused—had been hard, as if he still did physical work. She hadn't realized till just now that she'd noticed.

But then there was the fit of his pin-striped suit. Susannah still had trouble reconciling that suit with the Marc she remembered.... Not that it mattered, she told herself firmly. It was a waste of time to speculate about a man from a far distant past. A man who could never be important to her again.

She'd do her job, and Marc would go back to his regular life, wherever it was. And whatever—and whomever—it involved.

In the end, Susannah was glad her presentation was scheduled for Friday afternoon, because it forced her to push the entire problem of Cyrus's paintings out of her mind. Instead, she spent the day concentrating on how to carry off a widespread recall of child safety seats without creating a national panic, and—less important but perhaps even more difficult—how to present her strategy to the manufacturer without causing an uproar which might cost Tryad future business.

By late afternoon, she'd managed both, and she celebrated by taking a cab back to Tryad's offices. The work was far from over, but with all the plans approved and in place, the rest would be relatively easy.

She'd actually forgotten Cyrus and the paintings until she reached into her handbag to pay the cabbie and her fingertips touched a small square envelope. Rita had handed it to her as she went out the door for her presentation, saying it had just been delivered by a courier service. Susannah hadn't even opened it, just shoved it into her bag. But she knew what was inside; through the heavy paper, embossed with Joseph Brewster's name, she'd been able to feel the shape of a key.

The key to Cyrus Albrecht's house, no doubt. Well, Monday would be soon enough to figure out how she was going to handle the problem of setting a fair value on Cyrus's art collection *and* keep Pierce and the museum's board happy.

The good news, she told herself, was that by Monday, Marc Herrington would have gone back to—wherever it was he'd come from. In fact, she thought he was probably gone already, or Joe Brewster wouldn't have sent her a key. Not that she was planning to check; she deserved a peaceful weekend.

And the sudden drop in spirits she was suffering at the moment was an aftereffect of hard work and stress, of relief, of worry about how she was going to pull off this assignment. It had nothing to do, she was certain, with whether or not Marc Herrington was still in Chicago.

She handed the fare over to the cabbie and reached for the door handle, only to feel it slide away under her hand as the door was opened from outside.

Another commuter, she thought, *anxious to pick up a cab at rush hour. At least he could wait till I'm out!*

But the odds were that anyone hailing a cab in this neighborhood was a client of Tryad's, so she swallowed the tart comment she'd have liked to make and smiled instead. "I'm glad I happened along just when you needed the cab," she said sweetly, and planted one foot on the curb.

"Perfect timing, in fact," a rich baritone answered.

Susannah's heel went out from under her and she tumbled back against the cab's seat.

"Except that since you're here, I don't need a cab," Marc went on reasonably. "May I offer you a hand, Susannah, since you seem to be having trouble getting out on your own?"

Today he looked more like the Marc she remembered—his jeans worn to pale blue and clinging to narrow hips, his pullover shirt emphasizing the breadth of his shoulders and the strength of his arms. Without apparent effort he almost lifted Susannah out of the cab, then stood with a hand still on her arm as if to steady her as he waved the driver away.

"What are you doing here?" As soon as the words were out, Susannah wanted to bite her tongue off; as opening gambits, that was about the worst she could think of.

"Don't you think we have a few things to talk about?"

Pierce had said something yesterday about Marc looking at her like a hungry wolf. Susannah couldn't see anything of the sort, herself. And she could detect nothing suggestive about his voice; his tone was perfectly level, and in fact he didn't sound particularly interested. The combination made her feel a great deal more sure of herself, and she attacked. "I can't imagine what we'd have to discuss. If you happen to be wondering what makes a public relations person qualified to appraise an art collection—"

"Oh, nothing so dull as that," Marc said. "Besides, who am I to question your aptitude for the job? Growing up in such a privileged family, one of the Northbrook Millers—I imagine you absorbed more about art with your infant formula than I know now."

A privileged family. For a moment, she wondered if there was the smallest hint of sarcasm in his tone. But Marc didn't know. Marc couldn't know...

He added, very gently, "I left a message for you with your receptionist, that I just wanted to talk over old times. She seemed to think you'd be disappointed to have missed me."

Just my luck, Susannah thought, *to have caught him on the way out. If I'd been five minutes later—just five minutes...*

The white lace curtain on Mrs. Holcomb's bay window next door didn't just flutter as it usually did when anything of interest happened on the street outside. This time the lace was actually folded back, and Susannah didn't think she was imagining the shadowy face which appeared behind the glass.

And if Mrs. Holcomb could see this very interesting conversation, so could Rita and Alison—if they happened to look out the window. And if Susannah walked into Tryad with Marc Herrington in tow, she might as well issue engraved invitations to a grilling, with herself on the barbecue spit.

She sighed. "There's a little restaurant around the corner. How about a cup of coffee?"

"I thought you'd never ask. Shall I carry your briefcase?"

Susannah surrendered it, and pretended not to notice when Marc offered his arm. She spent the couple of minutes' walk debating with herself. Had he always been a gentleman, or was that, too, something new? At eighteen, in the midst of a revolt against her parents' values—a rebellion which had come a little later but no less violently than that of most teenagers—would she even have noticed such things as courtly manners?

The same waitress who had been working at breakfast hour on Monday brought their coffee, and dimpled when Marc thanked her.

Susannah stirred cream into her coffee and said, "Old times, you said. All right—you go first. What have you been up to for the last eight years? What are you working at these days?"

"I'm still in manufacturing." Marc stretched out his hands—long fingers arched, each knuckle tensed. It was a gesture Susannah remembered seeing often, though the reason for it was less vivid in her mind. She vaguely recalled that he'd said something about the need to keep his hands flexible, for the work he did...

"Welding must be paying better these days," she said crisply, "for you to afford to dress like that. The suit you were wearing at the funeral yesterday—"

"Did you like it? I bought it just for the occasion."

"Is that why the funeral was delayed—to let you go shopping? Nice that you thought that highly of Cyrus."

"I didn't, particularly. I never met the man in my life."

That much didn't surprise her, but it chipped away at her original theory that Cyrus's mysterious heir was also his son. To the best of Susannah's recollection, Marc had had a perfectly serviceable set of parents... "I must admit I'd like to know how your mother met him."

"I'll have to ask her sometime. As long as we're talking about families, how's your daughter, Susannah?"

The question came at her like a curve ball, hanging just out of reach for an impossibly long time, taunting her. She wasn't shocked, exactly; she'd been half expecting something of the sort. Why had he fixed on a girl? "I don't have a daughter."

"Really? It seemed a perfectly reasonable conclusion. A professional office probably wouldn't provide hopscotch layouts on the front walk for clients' children— at least, not the sort of firm yours obviously is. And since hopscotch is not only a little girl's game, but is most fascinating to girls exactly the age yours would be..."

"Very logical," she admitted. "Very reasonable. And very wrong. The neighborhood girls like to play there. It's the widest and flattest walk around."

"A son, then?"

"Sorry to disappoint you."

Marc was stirring his coffee. "Oh, I couldn't be any more disillusioned with you than I was eight years ago. I must admit, however, I'd like to know what happened. I expected, after you told me that you hadn't married after all, that you'd still be trying to convince the world your child was also mine, and I'd been too much of a bum to marry you. Naive of me, wasn't it, to think that? Of course the Northbrook Millers would figure out a neater, easier way. What was it, Susannah? A convenient miscarriage?'' The spoon didn't stop moving in concentric circles as his gaze lifted to meet hers. ''A very private adoption?''

''As you pointed out yourself, it's none of your business.''

''Perhaps I should ask Pierce.''

''He doesn't know.''

''In that case, it might be even more interesting to compare notes.''

''Be my guest. Is there anything else you wanted, Marc?''

''Oh, I could think of a few things.''

Susannah took that with a grain of salt. ''Then I doubt I'll see you again.''

''What makes you think that?'' Only mild interest spiced his voice.

She shrugged, but the gesture turned out, despite her best efforts, to be more like a shiver. What was there about his gentle, even voice that scared her so? ''I assume you'll go back to your life. There must be things you can't walk away from.''

''You mean things like the job, the mortgage, the wife, and the kids?''

Wife? *Kids?* But why shouldn't he have married? Susannah could think of no good reason.

Her gaze went straight to his left hand, cupped easily on the plastic surface of the table. He wore no wedding ring, and there was no telltale pale band where one might have rested in the past....

Marc followed her gaze. His eyes narrowed, and he stretched out his hand toward her. ''So you still have wedding rings on the brain. Sorry to disappoint you.''

"I see," she said. "The machinery you work around makes a ring dangerous. Catch it wrong, and it could tear off your finger."

"True," he said. "Besides, it makes a handy excuse not to wear a ring. I think you've misunderstood, though. I'm not going back for a while. The wife—well, you know how these things go. A break sounds like a very good idea. And as for the kids—I don't know why you'd assume that one can't walk out on children, Susannah, considering your own record."

She was too numb to be shocked.

"And as far as the job and the mortgage—well, it's such a large inheritance, you see, that neither of those things matters much just now. Or at least it should be a tidy sum, if it's properly looked after and not left to a bunch of vultures."

"Meaning me?" Susannah managed to keep her voice steady, but it took enormous effort.

"Now why would you jump to the conclusion that I was talking about you?" Marc's tone was soft, almost caressing. "Right now, it just makes sense to stick around and keep my eye on things—and that's exactly what I'm going to do."

CHAPTER THREE

DESPITE the effort she'd made to convince herself that
Marc wouldn't—couldn't—stay in Chicago, Susannah
wasn't really surprised. It *was* a sizable estate. One had
only to walk into Cyrus's house to realize that.

She could imagine the impact that house had had on
Marc—the gleaming furniture, the solid walnut staircase,
the art on the walls...even if he didn't care for the sub-
jects, he must have realized the paintings themselves
were far above poster quality.

She could still remember his low whistle when he'd
gotten his first glimpse of the Miller's house, on that
never-to-be-forgotten weekend when Susannah had
brought him home on her Thanksgiving break from college to meet her family. If her parents' house, spare and
modern and all stainless steel and glass, had evoked that
sort of response, Susannah could imagine the way he'd
reacted to Cyrus's exuberant Victorian.

And, once realizing the probable worth of his legacy,
of course Marc would stay, watchful and protective, until
everything was settled and the cash safely in his hands.
He had no reason, after all, to trust Joe Brewster—or
anyone else. And beside the magnitude of Cyrus's estate,
a welder's income must look like peanuts, easily tossed
aside.

"Of course," she said coolly. "It only makes sense
to protect oneself."

Marc's eyes narrowed. "Thank you for sharing your
personal philosophy."

Susannah opened her mouth to say that she hadn't
been talking about herself, and then decided the point

wasn't worth explaining. She wasn't going to convince him with mere words. Not that she *wanted* to convince him; what did it matter what Marc thought of her?

"You're quite right," Marc went on thoughtfully. "And I'll certainly keep your advice in mind as this process unfolds. I wonder how long it will take. A year, maybe.... Another cup of coffee?"

Susannah shook her head. The motion felt like forcing rusty machinery to move against its will; the tension in her muscles was the worst she'd ever felt. *A year?* Of course he was right; an estate the size of Cyrus's would take forever to untangle.

On the other hand, perhaps she'd overestimated her part of the work. It would take time, of course, but much of it would be spent in libraries, not with the paintings themselves. She might not run into Marc much at all.

"Very well," Marc said. He slid out of the booth.

Susannah made the mistake of looking up at him. He seemed incredibly tall, broad-shouldered, strong, as he stood there. He wasn't frightening, exactly, but it was only sensible to be watchful. And she was certainly that; there seemed to be as much wariness circulating in her veins as blood.

"I'll see you Monday, then," he said. "Unless you'd prefer to spend the weekend with me?"

Susannah had turned, reaching for her handbag and briefcase. Her head snapped up once more; all her inner alarms shouted, *Danger.*

"Inventorying Cyrus's pictures, of course," he added smoothly. "Good heavens, Susannah, your eyes look like the Gulf of Mexico—the same shade of blue-green, and nearly as big. What did you think I meant?"

Susannah knew perfectly well what he'd meant. He'd meant for her to think that he was offering a weekend full of passion. And of course she'd fallen straight into the trap by reacting as she had. In fact, the only real question was what he'd *truly* been offering—an honest-to-goodness illicit encounter, or only a chance to make a fool of herself once more for his entertainment.

The old Marc wouldn't have thought of either alternative, she knew. The young man she had known had been ardent—no doubt about that; she had yet to meet another man who could knock her socks off with a kiss as Marc had been able to. But he'd also been respectful, sometimes to the point of being quaint. He'd almost worshiped her; he would never have made that careless, offhand reference to sleeping together. And he would never have baited her, or embarrassed her.

The new Marc was cynical, sardonic, distrustful—and far more dangerous. The sooner Susannah stopped thinking of the man he'd once been and started handling him as she would a jar of nitroglycerine, the better off she'd be.

Still, she spent most of the weekend turning the whole thing over in her head—grooming the acid barbs she wished she'd thought of earlier and fretting about what Monday would bring. Why had she committed herself to showing up at Cyrus's house on Monday, anyway?

Stupid question, of course. She'd been so anxious to squash the idea of a weekend together that she'd actually set the time herself. Was that, perhaps, what he'd been after all along? Making sure that she wouldn't simply put off the appraisal indefinitely, in the hope that he'd give up and go away?

Maybe it's better to get it over with, she told herself. Cyrus's collection might be large, but it couldn't be all that difficult to make a list, and then the rest of her work could be done in the Dearborn Museum's library.

But even positive thinking didn't make it easier to look forward to Monday morning.

The day started off badly; she was late to the partners'

breakfast. *And no excuse in sight,* Susannah told herself grimly as she pulled open the restaurant door and started toward the reserved back booth. There hadn't been a convenient bake sale along her way, as there had been last week. And she simply couldn't confide in Alison that the reason she was late was because she'd done her hair three different ways before settling on a severe French twist. To say nothing of the problem of getting dressed...

The dress she'd put on first had felt too short today—though she'd worn it to the office a dozen times before, and no one had ever looked askance at the hemline. Her second choice had been a suit which boasted a camisole blouse—too flimsy and clingy, she'd decided, and asked herself how she'd overlooked for so long the fact that the fabric was almost transparent.

Because it isn't, she concluded. She was simply being super-sensitive, determined not to give Marc an easy target.

She took a deep breath and started talking before she'd even reached the booth. "Sorry to be late, Ali. You won't believe—" She broke off at the sight of the woman sitting across from Alison. "Kitty!" she shrieked in delight. "You came home!"

Tryad's third partner raised her well-groomed dark eyebrows. "There was doubt?" She turned to Alison. "She forgot I was coming back this week."

"It's not the only thing she's forgotten lately," Alison pointed out.

"That's true," Kit murmured. "How long have we been meeting at Flanagan's every Friday night to talk about the week?"

"Three years and...let's see..." Alison calculated. "Six months. Ever since we formed the partnership."

"And she's never forgotten before," Kit said.

Susannah sighed. "I didn't forget this time, either. I

mean, I didn't *really* forget. I got tied up, and you'd already left by the time I got to Flanagan's.'' It was perfectly true; she'd sat in this very booth over her empty coffee cup for half an hour after Marc had left. By the time she'd remembered it was Friday and made a mad dash down to Flanagan's, Alison had come and gone.

''She got tied up,'' Kit said soberly. ''Now that's a story I'd like to hear.''

''And then there's the small matter of the clothes,'' Alison murmured. ''That's the plain navy blue suit she only puts on when we have to impress bankers and attorneys. I wonder why she's wearing it on an ordinary Monday.''

''Would you two knock it off? I'm here, you don't need to talk about me as if I'm not!''

''We're getting quite used to it,'' Alison pointed out. ''That's why we didn't file a missing persons report Friday night.''

''You were *both* there? Flanagan didn't tell me that.''

''Also,'' Kit added helpfully, ''we took into account the fact that Rita said the man in question didn't look like a serial killer.''

''A serial killer who looked like one would never get to his second victim,'' Susannah snapped.

Kit leaned forward and put her elbows on the table. ''So give, Sue. Who's Marcus Herrington?''

''Just back from your honeymoon,'' Susannah mourned, ''and you're already interested in another man?''

''That's no answer to my question.''

''I hoped you'd notice that.'' Susannah called the waitress over. ''I'd like tea this morning, please, Carol. Nothing else.''

Kit relented. ''All right, you don't want to talk about him. We can take a hint—can't we, Ali?'' She reached across the table to pat Susannah's hand. "And any time you change your mind, darling, Ali and I are right here...just waiting."

Her tone was comforting, but there was a sparkle in her eyes which made the hair on the back of Susannah's neck stand up in alarm. Newly in love herself, Kit was apt to see romance in even the most unlikely situations...

And this, Susannah thought, *isn't just unlikely. It's impossible!*

The wrought-iron gates which blocked the front walk of Cyrus Albrecht's house were closed. The Queen Anne appeared even less friendly than it had on the day of Cyrus's funeral; despite the brilliance of a summer morning, the house looked eerie.

"Maybe I'll be lucky," Susannah muttered as she pushed open the front gate, "and it'll only be Cyrus's shade who's roaming the place!"

She rang the bell and listened with approval to the mellow, muted tones of the chimes somewhere deep within the house. But there was no answering movement, no rustle of clothing or click of heels, to greet her.

Susannah frowned, rang the bell again, and finally fumbled in her handbag for the key Joe Brewster had sent. "It figures," she muttered as she slipped it into the dead bolt lock. "I wasted a whole weekend fussing and fretting, and he's not even here."

The ominous warning beep of the alarm system startled her, and she fumbled for the sheet of instructions Joe Brewster had included on how to turn it off. It took precious seconds to find the control panel, in the closet under the stairs, and she sighed in relief when the last command was given and the beeping settled into silence.

Susannah wrinkled her nose at the Evans Jackson painting, still hanging in its place of honor. She wouldn't have been surprised, after what Marc had said about it, to find it out on the front step doubling as a Welcome mat.

What did surprise her was the incredible stillness of the house. The silence which fell after the alarm quieted was as thick as a blanket of dust which hadn't been disturbed in years.

Had Marc left after all? Perhaps he'd found himself missing his family...

Don't be silly, she told herself. That image fit a lot better with the Marc she'd known than it did with the new one. And yet, cynical and hard-edged as he'd become, she couldn't quite see him deserting a wife, a child or two or three... He'd never said, had he, how many there were?

And he's not exactly deserting them, either, she reminded herself. *He's taking care of their future by assuring himself that Cyrus's money is safe.*

She didn't quite know how she got to the top of the stairs, but when she found herself there she shrugged and pushed open the first door on the left of the long hall. A quick tour of the entire house was probably a good idea, she thought. Then she'd have a measure of the magnitude of the job, and she could pace herself accordingly...

What she'd thought was a bedroom wasn't. It was fitted up like a study instead, with a pair of leather armchairs by the fireplace and a huge desk which sat with its back to the morning light streaming in the window. And behind the desk, slumped over the blotter...

Susannah gasped. All she could see was the side of Marc's head and a wine-red terry bathrobe, pulled taut across his shoulders in what looked like a painfully unnatural pose. And was that a patch of something darker below the shoulders...?

She took two hasty steps toward the desk, trying to peer over its bulk to get a better view of the dark patch, and gave a little scream when Marc sat up, a torn sheet of paper in his hand.

"Good morning, Susannah," he said pleasantly, without looking at her. He inspected the sheet of paper, put it down on the blotter, and stood up, moving around the side of the desk.

Susannah's heart was still pounding erratically, and her brain refused to believe that he was all right. "I thought..." Her throat was so constricted she could hardly force the words through. "I thought you..."

The dark patch which she had seen on his shoulders fell now on the single page. Against wine-red terry it had looked like dried blood. Against the white paper the spot was definitely blue.

Blue? she thought in astonishment.

She glanced up at the stained-glass panel in the top of the tall window, and sighed. Directly in the center was a medallion of cobalt-blue glass. In the bright sunlight it glowed like a sapphire. Mixed with wine-red, its brilliance muted by the rough fabric... No wonder the combination had fooled her. It *had* looked just like blood.

"And you were coming, with hope in your heart, to check on whether I'd been stabbed with a letter opener? How thoughtful of you! Though you might want to change your bedtime reading, if this is the result."

Lucky for him, Susannah thought grimly, that there wasn't a letter opener on Cyrus's desk—the temptation might have proved too much for her. And where did he get off criticizing her reading material, anyway? Obviously he'd absorbed a few murder mysteries himself.

"It was the way you were sitting," she said coldly. "Or did you arrange yourself in that position on purpose when you heard me coming up the stairs?"

"Since I didn't hear you coming—no, I didn't. I was

trying to reach the farthest crack of the bottom drawer, because I could feel the edge of this paper stuck in it.'' He looked once more at the page spread on the desk blotter. ''And of course, after all that effort, it turns out to be nothing more than a laundry list.''

Now that her heartbeat had slowed, Susannah's irritation was growing. ''Of course there's the fact that you didn't answer the door, even though I rang the bell twice. So of course when I found you here, hunched over like that, I thought—''

His eyes were sparkling. ''Worried you, did it?'' He perched on the corner of the desk.

''Only because I'd be the obvious suspect,'' Susannah said tartly. ''How was I to know you were just too lazy to come down and answer the door?''

Marc shrugged. ''I knew you had a key, and I wasn't expecting anyone else.''

''Well, that much is obvious.'' Frowning in disapproval, she let her gaze drop from his face down the length of the terry robe. His shoulders looked even broader than they had under a pullover shirt. Perhaps it was partly because his chest was bared in a narrow V all the way to the belt knotted at his waist. A deeply tanned chest—which meant he'd taken full advantage of the Hawaiian sun. His big hands were clasped easily over one knee. Slim hips, well-muscled thighs—Susannah could tell because his pose had wrapped the robe tightly around his legs.

He moved, and the hem of the robe slipped. Susannah hastily raised her gaze to his face—and wished she hadn't. She was already a bit pink, she knew, and the gleam of unholy appreciation in his eyes brought a flood of color to her face.

The old Marc—not quite certain of his appeal, of himself—would have been uncomfortable showing off his body that way...

I was going to forget all about the old Marc, she reminded herself. She certainly had no time to worry about *him,* now that she had the new version to cope with!

"You're referring to my choice of clothes?" He smiled and shifted his weight once more. This time the bathrobe's belt slipped a fraction. "I don't know why you'd think I never entertain in my bathrobe," he mused. "But that's beside the point. The truth is I got absorbed in checking out Cyrus's files, and I forgot to watch the clock. Anyway, you should be glad I didn't rush off to get dressed the moment you rang the bell."

She didn't want to ask, but the question was out before she could stop herself. "Why?"

"Because you came straight to me, like a homing pigeon," he said gently. "And you'd have been even more embarrassed if you'd caught me—"

"In your natural state?" Susannah put every drop of sarcasm she could muster into her voice. "At least it's nice that one of us would have been embarrassed! Don't let me stop you from getting dressed now, by the way. Just tell me which bedroom you're using, and I'll avoid it."

Marc didn't move from the desk. "Know your way around up here well, do you?"

"It was sheer chance that I walked in here. I've never been upstairs before." Then she realized what he'd meant, and bristled. "How *dare* you suggest—" Words failed her.

Marc shrugged. "Your boss certainly implied you'd be—shall we say, cooperative?—where my new art collection is concerned. So I thought perhaps that held true when Cyrus still owned it, too."

What I wouldn't give right now, Susannah thought grimly, *for a letter opener!*

"I wouldn't throw that," Marc said calmly.

She looked down at the paperweight clenched in her hand. How had it gotten there?

He was right, though. The paperweight was a masterpiece in cut crystal, an art object in its own right.

The moment it took to set the paperweight carefully back on the desk was enough to reassert her self-control. He wanted her to blaze at him, to defend herself, to end up trapped in a corner of her own making—and she'd almost done it.

She said stiffly, "Pierce is not my boss. He's my client."

"Of course." Marc moved just enough to put his hands in his pockets. The robe's belt slipped a little more.

Susannah could almost hear his breathing, light and easy though it was. The house was incredibly still. "Didn't Cyrus have a staff?"

"Of sorts. I gave them all a vacation."

"Made you nervous to have them around, hmm?"

He smiled. "I'll give you two points for insight. They cramped my style somewhat, yes."

"I'm not surprised. If that's who was serving at the party after the funeral, not a one of them could be under seventy. Let the housekeeper see you in that bathrobe and you'd have a heart attack on your hands."

"Better that than an attack of the heart, I suppose," Marc mused. "Such inconvenient things—infatuations."

"I don't think you need to worry about that." She turned on her heel. "I'll be downstairs—working."

And with any luck, she thought, she'd be well along with the job before he was even out of the shower.

Marc took his time, and Susannah had worked her way through three rooms by the time she heard his step on the stairway. She didn't tense at the sound; it was almost a relief. Until she actually heard him, she hadn't been sure if he could come up behind her without warning—which would be a whole lot worse.

She glanced over her shoulder just as he came around the corner into the front parlor, and the sight almost took her breath away. She clutched at her clipboard and tried to look anywhere but at him.

With his dark hair still damp, wearing jeans even older than the ones he'd appeared in on Friday, a T-shirt which mocked big business, and loafers with no socks, he looked younger. He looked, in fact, very much like the old Marc. The Marc who had kissed her till she turned to mush, worshiped her...and ultimately turned his back on her.

And don't you forget it, Susannah ordered. She tried to focus her gaze on the painting above the mantel, but in that instant she couldn't have told whether it was a landscape or a portrait.

Marc came up behind her, so close that she could feel his breath stir the few loose hairs at the back of her neck. The scent of his soap reached out to torment her, more exotic somehow than the most expensive aftershave.

He reached over her shoulder and took the clipboard out of her hands. "What are you doing? Is this what you call an inventory?"

Susannah was puzzled. "It's a list, that's all, just enough for me to look things up. Type of painting, basic description, name of artist—what else do I need?"

"What about measurements? What about markings on the back of the canvas, or on the frame?"

"I doubt you'll find a sticker anywhere marked with the price Cyrus paid," Susannah said dryly.

"What about things that might lie underneath?"

"A modern image painted over an old masterpiece, you mean?" She shook her head. "These are pretty straightforward pieces of art. If there was anything like that, Pierce would know it."

"And I'm sure he'd rush to tell me," Marc said. His voice was as smooth as warm syrup.

She shot a suspicious look at him.

"Just as he so graciously filled me in on the value of the Evans Jackson in the front hall."

Susannah bit her lip. That was certainly one in the eye for Pierce. She only wished he'd been there to take the blow himself. "A fan of Evans Jackson, are you?"

"Of course not. I was completely honest about what I think of that painting."

"Then how do you know what his work's worth?"

Marc shrugged. "Read something in a magazine, I think. Or maybe I saw it on educational television."

"There was a 'Masterworks' piece on Jackson about a year ago," Susannah said slowly. "In fact, Pierce helped put it together. But somehow, that doesn't strike me as your kind of viewing."

"I remember now. There wasn't much choice. The baseball game I was trying to watch was held up till it stopped raining."

"I see," Susannah said. "And I suppose that's where you found out about old masterpieces hiding under modern paintings, too? I wouldn't worry about that, Marc. These days canvas is cheap, so artists don't have to paint over things."

"Even if it's something they should paint over," Marc agreed. "But I think you're changing the subject. I said we were going to do an inventory, and I mean a real inventory. So we'll have to take everything down, dust it off and look it over, and photograph not only the art itself but the frame, the back of the canvas, any markings…"

Susannah stared at him.

"Shall we take a coffee break before we start?"

Yes, Susannah wanted to say. *About a five-year-long coffee break.*

"Now that I think about it, I haven't had breakfast," Marc went on. "How about if I make us some sandwiches, we'll call it lunch, and afterward we can plunge in and do some real work." He pulled her painstakingly written sheets from the clipboard, wadded them up, and aimed them at the umbrella stand in the front hall just outside the parlor door. The makeshift ball rebounded off a rhinestone-embossed handle and slid out of sight in the depths of the stand.

Susannah protested, "But I had a lot of the work done already."

"No, it's better to start fresh. That way you won't be tempted to cut corners and try to write between the lines and in the margins, where notes can be misunderstood. Come on, you'll feel better after lunch."

She followed him to the kitchen, though she'd rather have run screaming out the front door.

The kitchen was surprisingly modern, considering the age of the house; the layout was convenient, the lighting good, and every appliance known to modern man was tucked into nooks in the rich wood cabinets.

Marc reached for a carving knife and a loaf of French bread, and pointed the knife at a high stool across the counter from the cutting board. "Sit," he ordered.

Susannah sat. "So what else do you know about art, besides Evans Jackson?"

He stopped slicing the top off the bread and looked at her thoughtfully. "I think that's called a leading question. Are you trying to find out what I know, so you'll have an idea how much to admit?"

"It's not, honestly. I'm curious."

He turned his attention back to the loaf. "There's beer, if you'd like some."

"No, thanks. If you don't want to answer—"

"—Then I won't. Cyrus had a wine cellar, too. There's a bottle or two in the refrigerator, I think. And would you hand me the cold cuts and lettuce while you're in there?''

At his direction, she practically emptied the refrigerator onto the counter in front of him. Almost buried at the back, behind the ham, cheese, tomatoes, green pepper, and all the other ingredients he was efficiently slicing and piling on the loaf of bread, she found a nice white wine. She poured herself a glass and sat sipping it as she watched the creation across the counter grow to immense proportions.

Finally, Marc put the top back on the loaf of bread, cut the whole thing in two, and put a plate in front of her.

Susannah looked doubtfully at the dimensions of the sandwich. "This looks delicious, Marc, but—''

"Oh, it is. Spend enough years packing lunches to take to work and you get pretty good at it.''

She could detect nothing in his tone but an acknowledgment of fact. That was one of the things which had attracted her to him in the first place; some of her college friends had looked down on his job and thought it menial. But Marc had always been proud, and he'd never tried to hide what he was. If he was going to be a welder, he'd be the best damn welder anywhere around...

The lump which suddenly formed in Susannah's throat threatened to choke her. She'd never liked the idea that Pierce had tried—was still trying—to put something over on Marc, but she couldn't stay quiet any longer.

She gathered up her sandwich and held it, without even trying to take a bite. It was almost too big for her hands, to say nothing of her mouth.

"Marc, there's something I have to tell you.''

He brought his plate around the counter and sat down next to her. The only sign of interest Susannah could detect was a quirk of his left eyebrow. "If it's your boss's clumsy attempt to get the Evans Jackson by running it down...."

"As I said, he's not my boss. And it's more than that." She set her sandwich down and took a deep breath. "Cyrus had agreed to donate his art to the Dearborn Museum."

Marc's eyebrow rose a little higher. "Joe Brewster hasn't said a thing about that."

"It does seem odd, doesn't it, that Cyrus wouldn't have told his attorney?"

"Damned odd. And I haven't found anything in his papers, either."

"No," Susannah admitted. "It hadn't gotten to that stage yet. It was an agreement in principle. But I assure you, he *had* agreed. I only met Cyrus a couple of times, but he'd even talked to me about it."

"Though he hadn't told his attorney. Let me get this straight, Susannah. You expect me to take your word for it and hand over—did you say the whole collection?"

"Yes. I mean, yes, he'd agreed to give us the whole collection. And no, I don't expect you to donate it. But I thought if you knew what Cyrus intended, that you might..."

He turned his head to look at her. It wasn't surprise she saw in his eyes, or amazement. She didn't quite know what the expression was, but she knew it wasn't promising for her cause.

Susannah could feel herself bogging down. The words which had seemed so sensible, so persuasive, just moments ago now felt like cold honey—stiff against her tongue. Her effort was going to do no good; she knew that now. But there was no way to make a graceful retreat. "I thought, to honor his wishes, you might let us have it at a price we can afford."

"But why should I honor his wishes?" Marc said softly. "Even if I was certain they *were* his wishes? If he didn't feel strongly enough about this so-called gift to bother to write down his intentions, or even tell Joe..." He paused and tilted his head to listen, then sighed. "Damn. I knew I'd forgotten something."

Susannah could hear what sounded like a branch brushing against the back door, a low moan, and a single plaintive bark. "I didn't know Cyrus had a dog. He didn't seem to be a dog sort of person."

"I suppose," Marc said wryly, "that he was intended to be a watchdog." He pushed his plate aside and went to open the door. A streak of red-gold flashed through the door and resolved itself into an Irish setter who reared up to plant his front paws on Marc's shoulders and take a swipe at his face with a long wet tongue. With that greeting taken care of, he sniffed the air and headed straight for Susannah. He sat squarely on her foot and grinned up at her, tongue lolling.

"See what I mean?" Marc said. "He's dumb—but loyal. And since he seems to have decided I'm the new Cyrus in his life..."

"Well, that doesn't explain him taking to me." Susannah tried to shift her foot from under the dog. "Or perhaps it's my sandwich he's after."

"No—I've vouched for you, in O'Leary's opinion, just by letting you into the house."

"I see why you have your doubts about him as a guard dog. Wait a minute—O'Leary, as in Mrs. O'Leary's cow that started the great Chicago fire?"

"It seems fitting, don't you think? It doesn't say much for his perceptions of course, that he's positive you wouldn't do anything nasty."

"Thanks," Susannah muttered. "If you're telling me you think I made this story up—"

"Oh, no. I'm sure there's truth in it." He sat down again and reached for his sandwich. "And if that *was* what Cyrus intended..." His voice trailed off. "You know, we just might be able to work something out."

Susannah's jaw dropped.

"Yes," Marc said meditatively. "Why don't you tell your boss I'll give it some thought, and get back to him?"

Susannah couldn't even talk. But it didn't matter; she was so pleased at the way her gamble had paid off that she wouldn't have bothered to correct him, anyway.

CHAPTER FOUR

SUSANNAH was dead tired by the time she got back to Tryad that evening. Her plain navy suit had turned almost charcoal-colored with dust, and her feet hurt. Her shoes weren't extremely high-heeled, but they hadn't been designed for standing at the foot of a ladder for hours on end, taking notes and handing things up and down. That was the job Marc had assigned her when she pointed out that her skirt—though it was almost the longest in her wardrobe—wasn't designed for climbing around like a monkey.

As soon as she'd made the comment, Susannah had regretted it, for Mark took a long and appraising look. He surveyed every inch of her, from shining blond French twist to plain dark blue pumps. Then he made a noise which might have been agreement, and climbed atop the ladder to take down the first painting.

Tomorrow, she decided, she'd wear jeans and take her turn. It was the least she could do, considering the concession Marc had made about the collection—even if her reasoning had more to do with that look he'd given her than with splitting the work fairly.

It had, after all, been a major concession for him even to consider acting on the wishes Cyrus had neglected to put in writing. And to do so on her word alone...

If that's what Cyrus intended..., Marc had said. But he hadn't sounded at all doubtful or sarcastic, as he would if he'd thought she was trying to put one over on him. He'd been contemplative, instead—as if he was thinking over how to balance all the factors so everyone would, when it was all over, feel fairly treated.

The hopscotch board on Tryad's front walk was faded now, and the numbers had smudged, but the outlines were still clear enough to see. Susannah danced across the design as enthusiastically as any eight-year-old, waved at Mrs. Holcomb's bay window, and arrived on the porch, fumbling for her key, just as Kit opened the front door.

"It must have been quite the day," Kit said calmly, and stepped back into Rita's office.

"As a matter of fact, it was." Susannah frowned. Rita's office was dark, her computer neatly hooded. That was no surprise, considering the hour, but she hadn't expected anyone to still be around. "Why are you here so late?"

Kit held up a handful of envelopes. "Trying to dig out from under all the paper that was waiting for me. Did you see the way my in-basket was heaped? And this is just the ordinary stuff, since you and Alison took care of the important things while I was gone."

Reminded of her own in-basket, Susannah took a look and groaned. Much of what waited for her was pink message slips, covered in Rita's neat handwriting with the details of calls which would have to be returned. *When?* she wondered. If she was going to spend tomorrow on a ladder...

Kit grinned. "Don't grimace like that. I'd guess, from what Rita said, that two-thirds of those messages are from Pierce."

"Oh, in that case..." Susannah smiled at the thought of calling him with the news. He'd be more over-the-moon than she was, no doubt, to know that he might get his precious pictures after all.

Kit looked intrigued. "I wish Ali was here to see that smile. And she told me you weren't serious about him!"

"Well, she's right." The very idea was almost funny, Susannah thought. Once, she might have found Pierce alluring—but between his career and hers, there had never been time for anything to develop, so the initial attraction had slid into casual friendship instead. Now Susannah was glad. After Cyrus's funeral, she'd seen a side of him she'd never glimpsed before, and she didn't much like the acquisitive, sly-as-a-fox Pierce.

"Which leads me to wonder exactly why," Kit murmured. "It wouldn't have something to do with Marcus Herrington, would it?"

"Of course not."

Kit looked amused at the vehemence in Susannah's tone. "Whatever you say, darling." She stacked the last of her outgoing mail on Rita's desk, murmured a goodnight, and slipped out the front door just as the telephone rang again.

Susannah sat down at Rita's desk to answer. "Tryad Public Relations."

"Susannah?" Pierce said, eagerly. "How did it go?"

"Very well, I think. We inventoried two rooms."

"Is that all?"

"Believe me, it was a full day's work. And also—don't get your hopes up too much, Pierce, but Marc said he might consider a deal."

She was so sure he'd yell in delight that Susannah hastily moved the phone away from her ear. But Pierce sounded more calculating than surprised. "The question, of course, is what kind of a deal. If we start too low, we'll lose him, but I don't want to offer enough to make him think he can hold us up for a fortune, either."

"*And thank you for doing a good job, Susannah,*" she said. "Oh, think nothing of it, Pierce. You're welcome. I was happy to do it."

"What? Oh, sure. Just don't give him any big ideas of what things are worth."

"I thought the actual valuations were going to be your department."

"Of course, so be subtle. Don't lay it on too thick, and don't say anything definite that might contradict me."

Susannah rolled her eyes, thinking of the Evans Jackson. If that hadn't been laying it on thick...

"And start feeling him out about the terms he wants, too," Pierce went on. "Do anything you can to convince him to make them favorable for us. Flatter him, humor him, compliment him on his taste—whatever you can think of. The better he feels about himself the more likely he is to be cooperative."

"Doesn't his opinion of the Dearborn matter more than his self-esteem?"

"Oh, I'll take care of that part. Bring him to the new show we're opening on Thursday night. That way all the board members can get to know him better."

"In other words, they can work on him, too?"

Pierce chuckled. "Plus he can see the Dearborn at its best—both the kind of operation we run and how Cyrus's collection would fit right in."

"Pierce, I know the new show isn't quite as off-the-wall as Evans Jackson, but I don't think it's Marc's kind of thing."

"Of course it isn't," Pierce said impatiently. "What would be? Calendar art and centerfolds?"

Susannah opened her mouth to mention the "Masterworks" series, and shut it again.

"*Rembrandt* probably wouldn't interest him," Pierce went on. "Take him to dinner first to soften him up."

"I'd really rather—"

"You're on expense account, Susannah. Make it somewhere nice. And don't spare the drinks, all right?"

The telephone clicked, leaving her with a sentence half formed. *Now that's a switch,* Susannah thought. In all the time she'd known Pierce, he'd never offered carte blanche for dinner expenses; he was as sensitive about

the museum's budget as he was his own, and money
wasted on food could not be spent on canvas and paint.
What was the world coming to?

At least Marc was already dressed when Susannah arrived at Cyrus's house on Tuesday, and he actually answered the door when she rang the bell. Beside him,
eagerly sniffing her hand, was O'Leary.

"I got the impression yesterday that the dog wasn't
allowed past the kitchen." Susannah tried to fend off a
wet tongue.

Marc spoke the dog's name, and O'Leary dropped to
his haunches and eyed his master woefully. "What do
you mean, *past the kitchen?* Before I came, he wasn't
allowed to set foot inside the house. I'm training him—I
don't see the point of having a dog at all if it isn't well-
behaved enough to go anywhere I do."

"Oh, that ought to make the staff very happy,"
Susannah said dryly.

Marc shrugged. "Then perhaps their vacations will
turn out to be longer than expected."

"That's a bit heartless, don't you think?"

"Now if that isn't a case of the pot calling the kettle
black...."

Susannah felt herself coloring. She'd forgotten that he
still seemed to think she'd simply disposed of an inconvenient child.

"Which reminds me, I haven't yet asked about the
rest of your family," he went on. "Come on back and
have a cup of coffee and tell me all about your parents."

"I'd much rather go to work."

His eyes were brilliant. "Does that mean there's
something you don't want to tell me?"

"Of course not." It wasn't the truth, of course, but
surely spending one holiday weekend long ago with her
parents didn't entitle him to a blow-by-blow description

of everything that had happened to the Millers since. "I've had my coffee already, and I'd like to get this job done as soon as possible."

His gaze slid slowly down the length of her, lingering on the way her jeans hugged her hips. Obviously, she thought, the change from skirt to pants hadn't made as much difference as she'd hoped it would.

"I see you're at least prepared to work today," he said finally. "Why the hurry, though? Eager to finish so you won't have to be around me?"

"Herrington, your ego's grown as big as New Jersey. It's not very attractive, you know."

He looked thoughtful. "Did you really like me better the other way? What a shame I didn't realize it then. I've believed all this time that you were so determined to have a wedding that you didn't care who the groom was—and I just happened to be the unlucky guy who was closest when you decided to make your announcement."

The comment stung as sharply as a slap. "I'd never have gone through with it," she said coolly.

"Why not? You think conscience would have reared its ugly head?"

"Not exactly. It's because worship gets to be a bit cloying after a while."

"I'm glad to know it. Not that you're likely to have the problem again, at least where I'm concerned."

You're supposed to be humoring him, Susannah reminded herself. *Flattering him. Making him feel good about himself... As if he needed any help in that department!*

"Anyway," she said firmly, "to go back to the original question—I'm in a hurry to finish because I have other clients and projects waiting for my attention."

He looked a bit doubtful, Susannah thought. And she must look annoyed—which wasn't going to get her anywhere at all. She forced a note of conciliation into her voice. "And I'm not trying to avoid you, either. In fact, how would you like to spend Thursday evening with me?"

His eyes sparkled. "Sweetheart, I had no idea you—"

Susannah raised her voice a little. "The Dearborn's opening a new show that night with a cocktail party and reception, and I thought you'd like to see the museum and meet the staff and the board of directors."

"Frankly, I'd rather be grilled over a slow fire. How about you let me choose the entertainment instead?"

Susannah went straight on. "The show is a collection of present-day Chicago artists who—"

"I guarantee," he said almost under his breath, "that if you let me call the shots, *you* wouldn't feel as if you were being grilled over a slow fire."

Susannah pretended not to hear him, but it took more self-control than she'd believed she possessed. "They work in a variety of styles, so I think there will be some you like. And some of the artists will be there, too."

"All right."

His sudden capitulation made Susannah so suspicious she almost lost her balance. "You mean you'll come?"

"Sure. I said I would, didn't I?"

"Why?" she said baldly. She tried frantically to retrace her line of argument, wondering what on earth had convinced him. "The chance to meet the artists?"

"Oh, no. I do want to see what the place looks like, you're right about that. And surely if there's a crowd your pal Pierce won't be able to give me a guided tour of every piece the museum owns."

She couldn't decide if having Pierce declared to be a best friend was better or worse than the misunderstanding about him being her boss, but she wasn't about to argue the point. And she couldn't take exception to his assessment of Pierce, for Marc wasn't far off track—

given half a chance, Pierce would go overboard in showing him around.

"It is nicer to look around at one's leisure," she said. "Good. That's settled, then."

Marc grinned. "I don't know about leisure. I expect my survey of the museum will take—oh, about ten minutes. And then I can devote the rest of the evening to surveying you."

She must have looked as if she'd swallowed a lemon, for he lifted both eyebrows and said solicitously, "But, Susannah, you *did* invite me. Isn't that what you had in mind? Making sure I had a guide who's worth looking at when the pictures aren't?"

After that, Susannah thought Marc should consider himself lucky not to have found a letter bomb bearing her fingerprints in the next day's mail. At least, she told herself, she hadn't already asked him to dinner by the time he'd really started pushing buttons—and she had no intention of repairing the omission.

She'd be the bait to get him to the opening, if that was the only way. But Pierce or no Pierce, she was darned if she'd wriggle onto the hook any earlier than she had to.

However, when Thursday afternoon came and almost went without Marc referring to the opening, Susannah was beginning to be perturbed. Surely he wouldn't stand her up at the last minute, would he?

She typed into her laptop computer the final details about the last of the paintings Marc had taken down from the dining room walls, and rubbed her eyes. She couldn't do any more until they'd hired a crew; all the remaining frames were too large for one person to move.

"Tired?"

She jerked upright in her chair as Marc spoke from directly behind her. It wasn't fair, Susannah growled to herself. He could walk so quietly that even the faint hum of the computer was enough to mask his movements. If it wasn't for the dog who was nearly always at his heels, she'd never hear Marc. And since she hadn't seen him since just after lunch, when he'd retreated to the upstairs study to continue looking for bills of sale, receipts, or records of what Cyrus had paid for each individual painting, she'd let her guard down.

"Maybe in that case," Marc went on, "we should just pass on the party tonight."

Susannah looked up at him with a blend of innocence and malice. "If you'd rather have a private tour, I'm sure Pierce would be happy to arrange it when he can give you his full attention for several hours."

"I think," Marc said pensively, "that's called being wounded with one's own ammunition. All right, let's go."

"But not dressed like that, surely."

Marc glanced down at his T-shirt, a white-on-black creation which reproduced the signatures of every major artist in the western world. "Why not? It's artistic."

"For one thing, it was created as a fund-raiser by one of the museums which competes with the Dearborn for art, visitors, and money."

"Really? If you insist, I'll take it off."

Before Susannah could protest, he'd pulled the shirt over his head, baring a broad chest which more than lived up to the sample she'd seen a few days ago under his terry robe. The muscles in his arms weren't bad, either, Susannah had to admit; every easy movement spoke of strength, but unlike most of the body-builder types she'd known, he didn't appear tempted to strike a pose. It seemed as if he was completely unaware of himself.

He held the shirt out for inspection. "I don't know why they'd be upset with me, though. I bought this at the Salvation Army thrift store, so the museum didn't get any money from me.''

''Believe me, I'd have no trouble convincing the Dearborn's board of *that!*''

Marc grinned. ''But if you insist, I'll see what I can come up with instead.''

As soon as he'd gone upstairs, Susannah locked herself in the downstairs powder room for a quick transformation. Her tailored linen blouse went into the side pocket of her briefcase, to be replaced by a lacy camisole. A touch of extra eye shadow, a gold necklace, and a pair of earrings which sparkled through the curtain of blond hair made all the difference in turning her simple dark green suit from office garb to evening wear.

She was waiting at the foot of the stairs when Marc came down, with the ever-present O'Leary right behind. He paused halfway, as soon as he saw her, and murmured, ''But my dear—you're so eager!''

''Only to see what you thought would be proper for the occasion.'' She couldn't fault his appearance, however. Though his suit was the same one he'd worn to Cyrus's funeral, he'd substituted a brighter tie and a pale blue shirt with—she checked—no monogram.

He followed her gaze to his cuff. ''If you're looking for initials, that shirt was an exception. It was a gift from a woman who seemed to think I'd forget my name without a constant reminder.''

''Your wife?'' Susannah said casually.

Marc smiled. ''Not even close.''

Which, Susannah thought, left her knowing nothing more at all.

In the car, she said, ''I'm all caught up with the paintings. I thought I'd ask Pierce tonight if he can recommend a crew to move the rest. It's only sensible to be careful who you let into the house.''

"Yes," Marc said thoughtfully. "That had occurred to me."

She shot a suspicious look at him, but she couldn't see even a gleam in his eyes which suggested hidden meanings.

He didn't take his eyes off the expressway traffic as he easily maneuvered Cyrus's big black Cadillac between a Mercedes and a delivery truck. "Since you're finished with that, I've got a pile of receipts for you to look at. The trouble is, a lot of them don't seem very clear—they list something more like a code number than an artist's name."

So much for Susannah's hopes of a quick end to the job. "I'll start cross-referencing tomorrow. If we can match some for certain, the others will be easier to figure out."

"That's why I thought writing down all the markings might be a good idea." There was a note of self-congratulation in his voice. Susannah had to restrain herself from sticking out her tongue at him. "But you know, in all the files I've searched—and believe me, Cyrus didn't throw away a single scrap of paper—I haven't found a mention of the Dearborn anywhere."

Susannah was surprised that he'd even looked. "Of course you haven't. I told you he hadn't put the fine points in writing yet."

"Fine points, nothing. I mean he doesn't even mention the general subject. Not so much as a hint." Marc's voice was low, each word separate and distinct.

Susannah's stomach seemed to turn over in slow motion. She could see the deal she'd been so proud of going up in smoke. Which was silly, for it hadn't been a deal at all; Marc had simply agreed to think it over and consider Cyrus's wishes...

Or was it something else which was bothering her?

Was it the idea that after all, he might think she'd made it all up?

No, she told herself. *That doesn't matter. It can't matter.*

"What about his calendar?" she said. "I'm sure he and Pierce had dinner together often."

"I haven't checked. But what would that prove—except that perhaps they liked the same restaurants? I think it's even possible, from some of the things Joe Brewster tells me, that Cyrus may have been pulling your pal Pierce's leg, and never intended to donate the pictures at all."

The car pulled up in front of the converted warehouse which housed the Dearborn Museum. *Great timing,* Susannah told herself. *He drops something like that on me two minutes before we walk into the museum and I have to face Pierce and the board...*

She closed her eyes against the hot prickle of tears. How unprofessional could she get? She could just imagine what Marc would have to say about it if she burst into sobs now.

The valet hired for the occasion appeared beside the car, and Marc came around the Cadillac to open Susannah's door. She tried not to look at him. "I guess you'll just have to think what you like, Marc."

He dropped into step beside her. "You're giving up so easily?"

The note of curiosity in his voice made Susannah want to hit him. "What do you expect me to do? Go forge a letter with the details, to try to convince you? I wouldn't know how to begin." She took a deep breath. "Whatever Cyrus intended, it can't be proved now. Take my word for it, or don't—but the paintings are yours, Marc. Do as you like with them."

"I will," he said softly. "You can be assured of that."

* * *

The opening was the biggest Susannah had seen in the Dearborn's three years in existence. No doubt that was partly because of the subject matter, she thought. Not only were most of the artists present, since they were all from Chicago, but they'd brought every friend and relative who lived in the metropolitan area, as well. And as for the remainder of the crowd... She wouldn't be surprised if Pierce had spent the whole week on the telephone, begging every person on the Dearborn's mailing list to show up tonight, to crowd the galleries.

"This looks like the hottest ticket in town," Marc said, but there was a note of irony in his voice, and he showed no other sign of being impressed. He seemed more interested in the tray of hors d'oeuvres offered by a white-coated waiter than in the art.

Susannah shook her head at the food; how could she possibly eat anything right now?

Marc was still making his selection when a matron with improbably auburn hair hurried up to them. "Susannah, dear, how are you?" But the matron had eyes only for Marc. "And this must be Mr. Herrington."

"Mrs. Adams is on the Dearborn's board," Susannah murmured.

Mrs. Adams flashed a smile. "How nice it is to meet you, Mr. Herrington! I hope you're enjoying our little exhibit?"

Susannah wished Pierce had overheard that description. He'd been working for the best part of a year on this *little exhibit*.

"Oh, I'm impressed," Marc said. "Very impressed."

Mrs. Adams looked triumphant.

Marc picked up another hors d'oeuvre. "Now this," he murmured, holding it up, "is what I call great art. Look at the way the cream cheese swirls around the pinwheel, and the idea of placing a single slice of green onion at the center... What do you suppose the artist meant to convey?''

Mrs. Adams's smile froze.

Marc grinned at her and drew Susannah farther into the gallery. She deduced that, with the advantage of superior height, he'd located the source of the waiters' trays, and perhaps the bar, as well.

''That wasn't very nice,'' she said. ''What had poor Mrs. Adams done to you?''

''It was what she was intending to do,'' Marc explained earnestly. ''I'd have been tied up all evening listening to a lecture and not seen a bit of the show.''

Susannah thought he probably wasn't referring to the paintings hanging on the oatmeal-colored walls of the gallery.

Marc flagged a passing waiter and handed Susannah a glass of sparkling wine. She took it, though she had no intention of doing much more than watch the bubbles rise. Tonight, she was obviously going to need every wit at her command.

Pierce came up, rubbing his hands. He glanced with approval from the glass in Marc's hand to Susannah.

As if, Susannah thought, *a glass or two of wine will affect Marc's decisions!*

''I hope you enjoyed dinner, Marc,'' he said.

Susannah bit her lip. Pierce had been consumed all week by the final details of the show, and she'd forgotten, in their one short conversation, to tell Pierce that she had no intention of taking Marc to dinner. She tried frantically to signal him to stop.

Pierce wasn't looking at her, however, but up at Marc. ''Did Susannah take you someplace nice?''

''Oh, yes,'' Marc drawled. ''Very nice. But she asked me not to tell you where we went. She said it's one of the best-kept secrets in Chicago and it'd be a shame if just anyone started to go there.''

Pierce's forehead wrinkled. "I see. Well, I hope you'll enjoy the show. If there's anything you'd like to know about, Marc, I'll be somewhere in the gallery all evening."

"I'll be sure to seek you out," Marc said.

Pierce went off to greet a group of newcomers.

"That was low," Susannah said.

"So was not following orders. Maybe I should have told him I didn't enjoy dinner nearly as much as I plan to enjoy dessert." The way his gaze slid down over her body made it clear he wasn't talking about food.

Susannah had just raised her glass to take a sip, and the sharp breath she drew made the wine's bubbles tickle her nose till she sneezed. "Dammit, Marc, would you cut out the suggestive nonsense?"

"But, Susannah, all I said was...." She glared at him, and he added, "Of course. If that's what you want."

She didn't trust him; the almost humble note in his voice didn't ring true for a second.

Not far away, Pierce had gathered a small group around him and raised his voice to interpret the plain black canvas on the wall behind him. Marc glanced toward him.

"If you'd like to go over and listen," Susannah said with a touch of malice, "don't let me keep you from it."

"Your pal Pierce is a fascinating study," Marc murmured. "He reminds me of that old saying—some are born great. Some achieve greatness. And then there are those who simply hire a public relations firm."

"That's *not* how the saying goes. And you don't need to be insulting about my job, either. I haven't said anything bad about yours, have I?"

"No," Marc admitted, "I have to agree you haven't. And I suppose public relations does fill a necessary spot in the world."

"Thanks."

"Where would people like Pierce be without it?"

Before she could answer, another of the female board members sailed up, kissed the air beside Susannah's cheek, and thrust a hand out at Marc. "We were just talking about you, a friend and I," she announced.

"What an honor for me," Marc said.

Susannah murmured an introduction, and the board member laid a red-nailed hand on Marc's arm and said, "She wondered if you were related to the Evanston Herringtons, and I said I didn't think you could be, but I'd just come and get to know you and find out for certain."

"I'm afraid not." Marc's tone was apologetic. "The Evanston Herringtons are far too upper class for me. Sort of like the Northbrook Millers."

Susannah held her tongue till the board member had fluttered off. "And that was even lower," she said.

"But true. That's puzzled me all along, you know. If you were going to pull a name out of thin air to be a father to your child, why make it so hard on yourself by choosing someone your parents thought was pond scum?"

There was no good answer to that. She could, Susannah supposed, admit that she'd suddenly gone berserk—but that was no answer. It might even lead to more questions. "Are you absolutely certain that was an insult, Marc? Pond scum always rises to the top."

Marc stared at her for a split second, then threw back his head and laughed.

She had forgotten how beautiful his laugh was. Like his voice, it was deep and musical, and it reached down into her heart and made her want to laugh with him. And the sparkle in his eyes made her ache. It had been so long since she'd seen that glint...

She couldn't face it, so she glanced out over the

crowd. Almost with relief she said, "Watch out. Board member off to starboard and on a collision course."

Marc turned his head to look. "The fussy lady with the Pekinese under her arm?"

"That's not a Pekinese, it's a mink stole. And don't ask me why she's carrying it around in June, because I don't know."

"Pity. I thought if dogs were welcome maybe next time I'd bring O'Leary."

Susannah shuddered. "Besides, she's not the one I was talking about. The board member is the tall thin man with the ascot tie."

"How many of these people are there, anyway?"

"An even dozen."

"Which means I still have nine to go?"

"I'm sure none of them will miss the opportunity."

The man with the ascot arrived. "Do you appreciate art, Mr. Herrington?"

"He certainly does," Susannah said sweetly. "He told me just the other day that his favorite television show is 'Masterworks.' After baseball, of course. And football, I suppose."

"And basketball and hockey," Marc added. "And a situation comedy or two. And the news channel, the weather report, and a couple of really good ads. Yes, sir, it's right at the top of my list. I even sent some money to 'Masterworks' once—enough to get their little magazine about what's going to be on the show next." He sounded quite proud of himself.

The board member lifted a hand to his ascot as if he were choking.

Susannah was almost in awe. Marc's instincts were superb; it was almost as if he *knew* this particular board member was one of the nation's biggest donors to public television—and therefore knew exactly how to skewer him.

"Of course," Marc went on, "I'm even more interested in certain select pieces of art. Cyrus's collection,
for example, will need proper care."

Two board members who were standing nearby
stopped talking in the middle of their sentences. The
silence which started with them rippled through the
crowd. Heads turned, gazes sharpened, bodies crept
closer.

It felt, Susannah thought, like standing on an island,
just she and Marc and the man in the ascot, surrounded
by still water.

"So I'm sure you'll be happy to know I've made a
decision about what to do with Cyrus's treasures," Marc
went on.

Susannah would have shielded her eyes—or clapped
both hands over her ears to shut out the announcement—but she couldn't move. *This is going to be awful,*
she thought. *He's going to tell them he's giving it to
some other museum...or auctioning it off...*

A murmur ran through the crowd. People pressed
closer, giving way only to let Pierce through into the
first rank of watchers.

Marc waited patiently for the whispers to die down.
"But because of Susannah, here, I've decided to give
the paintings to the Dearborn...."

A long, relieved sigh breathed through the gallery,
followed by a ripple of applause.

Susannah couldn't believe her ears. She stared at
Marc, frowning, wondering what miracle had moved
him to do this. She'd have sworn he had no such intention when they arrived—he'd as much as said so.
Nothing which had happened since could have inspired
the sort of confidence which this gift implied. And as
for giving credit to her... Susannah could think of absolutely nothing she'd done which could have changed
his mind.

She was still frantically thinking where the catch might be when Marc lifted a hand, and the applause died to a spatter and then to silence.

"One at a time," he added, and slipped his arm around Susannah's shoulders. "You'll get one of Cyrus's paintings...every time Susannah sleeps with me."

CHAPTER FIVE

UTTER silence fell on the Dearborn Museum. A matron somewhere in the back gave a shrill titter, an embarrassed half giggle which broke off uncertainly when the rest of the crowd didn't join in the joke.

The only person who was moving—or, Susannah thought, who was capable of moving—was Marc, who looked around the room with interest, eyebrows raised as if wondering what on earth he'd said that was so shocking.

She herself felt as if she'd been encased in concrete. Her chest was so tightly constricted she could hardly draw a breath, and she couldn't have stirred from the spot if fire had broken out directly under the soles of her shoes.

Marc said, "But I've interrupted the opening. How thoughtless of me to steal attention from the artists. Susannah, are you going to show me around? Or would you rather we—"

She could almost hear what was coming, and only an overwhelming desire to keep him from compounding her embarrassment forced her feet to move. She clutched his arm and tried to pull him toward the nearest painting.

For an instant she felt like a rowboat trying to tow an ocean liner. Then Marc cupped his hand over hers and fell into step beside her. "This is interesting," he said, and pointed at a splash of cobalt-blue paint. "What a sensual curve the artist has created right here—don't you think? In fact, the feeling of the entire painting is almost erotic—"

80

"Would you *quit?*" Her voice was low and hard-edged.

"If you'd like to go somewhere private and discuss it, Susannah, I'd be more than happy—"

"We *can't* go somewhere private, or every bloomin' person in this museum will think we..." How frustrating it was, she thought, not to be able to scream at him. An argument conducted in bare whispers was hardly satisfying. "Of all the outrageous stunts I've ever heard of, Marc Herrington, this one is the prizewinner."

"But I was just doing what you told me."

Susannah stared up at him in shock. "Oh, no. What could I possibly have said which gave you an excuse to embarrass me like that?"

"You told me to cut out the suggestive nonsense, so I did."

Susannah's mouth dropped open. He'd taken that careless, off-the-cuff order and willfully misunderstood it. He'd stopped being suggestive, all right; instead, he'd come straight out with the most outlandish proposition she'd ever heard.

One thing was certain—there was no point in talking to the man. He'd already proved that no matter what she said, he'd spin it around to his own advantage. Why give him more ammunition?

So she let him walk her from painting to painting, and half listened as he commented on each. And gradually, as the noise level in the gallery returned to normal, her breathing steadied and her sense of humor reasserted itself.

Of course, she thought, he hadn't meant it. He'd only said it because everybody associated with the museum had been treating him like some kind of barefoot hillbilly. *Do you even know what art is? Surely you're not fit to be related to the Evanston Herringtons? Are you able to appreciate our exhibit?* Those hadn't been the exact words, of course, but it didn't matter; the tone of condescension had been perfectly clear.

And no doubt Marc had realized that it wouldn't end tonight, either. Once formally introduced, the Dearborn's board would make it a point to encounter him, individually or en masse, in carefully arranged coincidences, in order to continue their campaign.

She almost didn't blame Marc for firing back. One thing about that grandstand statement: it had been precisely calculated to halt the board in its tracks.

But he hadn't meant it. This wasn't the Middle Ages, for heaven's sake...

Marc had asked twice if she was ready to go before she even heard him, and then Susannah stared up at him in disbelief. "I'm not leaving with you."

"Why not? You came with me, remember? Your car is parked in Cyrus's driveway."

"Who cares? I am not getting into a car with you. After everything you've said tonight—"

He held up his hand Boy Scout style. "I promise faithfully that I won't—what's that charming phrase your mother once used?—take advantage of you."

"If you ever try, you'll regret it. I can defend myself quite well. I'm just not walking out of this building with you in front of a zillion people." Head high, she descended the stairs to the front entrance.

She'd been correct about the crowd; dozens of people were already waiting in the museum entrance and on the sidewalk for their cars to be brought around. Half of them, Susannah saw, were eyeing her covertly. The other half weren't even pretending to hide their interest. "I'll ask the valet to call a cab."

Marc was no more than a step behind her. "I was taught it was only polite, once I'd taken a girl out on a date, to see her safely home."

Susannah glared at him over her shoulder. "This wasn't a date, so I absolve you of responsibility."

"All right," he said. "Call a cab. I'll tell everybody you're so sensitive about privacy that you're meeting me later at Cyrus's house."

He'd do it, too, she knew, and he'd probably enjoy it. And since it was, in a sense, the truth—even though the *later* he referred to would be tomorrow rather than tonight, and the occasion work rather than passionate love-making—Susannah had no doubt he'd say it with an absolutely straight face.

"Oh, come on, Susannah." For the first time, Marc sounded a bit exasperated. "Hold your head up, and you'll keep them wondering. Cower and they'll be on you like a pack of wolves. Didn't your society upbringing teach you anything at all—or weren't the playgrounds in Northbrook anything like the ones I grew up on?"

"Obviously not," she said crisply. "It would certainly never have occurred to me to suggest the sort of bargain that seems to spring quite naturally to *your* mind. All right—but you can take me straight home, because I'm not going back to Cyrus's house tonight."

"Why not? Don't you think O'Leary would defend your virtue?" Before she could answer, Marc added, "That's probably sensible. There's no point in going all the way west to pick up your car at this hour. Unless—"

"I'm certainly not spending the night with you."

Marc shrugged. "It never hurts to ask. I'll come into town and get you in the morning."

"You needn't bother. That's why Chicago has a train system."

The valet brought Cyrus's Cadillac around just then, and Marc's answer was lost in the purr of the engine.

With the museum crowd safely left behind, some of the tension in Susannah's body trickled away. She gave

Marc directions to her apartment and settled back for the ride.

He looked puzzled. "That neighborhood can't be too far from Lincoln Park."

"Congratulations. You're getting your Chicago geography straight."

"Oh, I went to the zoo last weekend, since you wouldn't have anything to do with me."

"With O'Leary underfoot, you felt a need for more animals? What's the big deal about where I live, anyway? It's close to Tryad, so I walk to work unless I know I'll need my car."

"Well, it's not a bad neighborhood. But somehow I expected Lakeshore Tower, or a condo on the Magnificent Mile. Something with a much grander address."

"We all have idiosyncrasies. Mine is that I'd rather have convenience than elegance."

"I'll bet your mother doesn't agree."

She didn't look at him. "As a matter of fact, she doesn't."

Her apartment was in a nondescript building almost the same proportions as a child's alphabet block, in the center of a middle-class neighborhood. The building was architecturally insignificant, and seeing it as if for the first time as the Cadillac pulled into the parking lot, Susannah couldn't help but wonder about Marc's impression.

She wasn't about to ask, however. "The parking's very restricted, so if you'll just stop in front of the building and let me get out..."

"But since your car isn't here," Marc pointed out, "why can't I use your space?"

Was there no way to outmaneuver the man? Susannah gave in and pointed out her reserved spot. "But I'm not inviting you in."

"Did I ask?" Marc's tone was mild. "It's late. You're tired. I have a long drive. Neither of us needs coffee at this hour... Have I missed any excuses?"

Susannah bit her tongue.

He pulled the building's front door open for her, but he didn't set a foot over the threshold. "Sleep well, Susannah. I don't expect to."

"Don't give me that guff, Marc. I don't see why you shouldn't sleep like a baby. Now that you know the paintings are perfectly safe—"

Marc drew her back onto the sidewalk and pushed the door shut. "Would you like to elaborate on that? If you mean they'll soon be in the hands of the museum—"

One at a time...whenever Susannah sleeps with me...

She felt hot color sweep over her face. "Of course that's not what I was going to say. I meant they're safe, from your point of view. After that display, Pierce and the board won't bother you anymore, and you can do whatever you want with the damned paintings."

"Not really." He didn't sound interested. "Since I've made an offer, I'm committed to the terms at least until—"

"Dammit, Marc, my virtue isn't something to be bargained for like a dowry, with me having no say in the matter!"

He sounded curious. "Who implied that you have nothing to say about it?"

"You did. That ridiculous arrangement you proposed—"

"But it's entirely up to you, Susannah. It's your choice."

His voice held a note of earnestness that scraped her nerves raw, because she didn't believe for a moment that he really felt that way.

"Either the Dearborn gets the paintings, or it doesn't," Marc said gently. "I'd rather it did, of course, because I would thoroughly enjoy carrying out the conditions of the donation. But I'll be a good sport about it, whatever you do. However, just to help you decide…''

He put both hands on her shoulders and drew her toward him.

She could have broken free, for his touch was gentle. But if she did, Susannah knew, he would never let her forget it. He'd imply that she'd been too afraid of her own desires to kiss him, too tempted by his offer to take the chance of losing control.

There was only one answer. It was just a kiss, after all. She'd suffer it, coolly and pleasantly, and prove that it meant nothing to her. That *he* meant nothing to her. He might have been able to kiss her senseless eight years ago, but he couldn't do it anymore.

She was wrong. He'd never been able to make her stop breathing, before.

The evening air had chilled, and at first his lips were deliciously cool against hers. Slowly, however, as his mouth moved with infinite care over her lips, her cheek, her temple, and back again, warmth began to creep through her. At first it was a comforting sort of heat, like a soft blanket on a cold night. But then the gentle warmth built gradually higher, hotter, till she could feel the crackle as her bones grew soft as ash, and she clung to him in an effort to stay upright.

What had he said, when she'd invited him to the museum opening? He'd implied that it would be torture. Like being grilled over a slow fire, that was it. And he'd told her that being with him would be nothing like that.

But he'd been wrong. Susannah knew, now, exactly how that grilling would feel. But it wasn't torture, exactly, except in the most exquisite sense. It was a delicious ache which cried out for a remedy only he could provide.

So this, she thought vaguely, *is his definition of being a good sport.* Making it impossible for her to see, hear, feel, taste anything but him. Knocking her off balance, till she was almost unable to stand without him, even with the support of the door at her back.

Leaving her alone. That was the most monstrously unfair thing of all...

The mere thought stunned her; the last gasp of common sense told her she should be glad he'd set her carefully aside and stepped away.

"Something to think about," Marc said. His voice was low and almost rough, as if he'd done a bit of damage to himself, as well. Or perhaps that, too, was a calculated part of the effect he'd succeeded all too well in creating—making her think that he'd been just as affected as she was.

He walked away, and she waited, just inside the lobby, until the Cadillac drew away before she climbed the stairs and walked down the long hall to her apartment. She didn't even turn on the lights, just threw herself down on the couch. Every nerve in her body was humming like a high-voltage wire.

"Damn," she said. "The man's *good.*"

Susannah wasn't surprised when not a single member of the Dearborn's board called her on Friday. She couldn't decide, however, if their silence was approving or eerie. Surely they hadn't believed Marc's nonsense—but shouldn't at least one of them have called to sympathize? Or had they been so embarrassed by the show he'd put on that they were pretending none of it had ever happened?

Marc didn't call, either. Not that she'd expected him to, really; it might be days before he realized that she'd meant what she'd said. Days before he really comprehended that a single kiss—stunning though it had been—hadn't changed her mind. Well, she could wait forever. She didn't think Marc could.

In any case, Susannah was grateful for the quiet. She spent the day in her office, catching up on projects which had been put off all week, and she was the first of the partners to arrive at their regular meeting at Flanagan's after the workday was finished.

She was stirring a glass of tonic water when Kit and Alison came in and took seats on either side of her.

"My goodness," Kit said. "There really *is* a Susannah Miller. After the better part of a week without a sighting, I was beginning to doubt my memory."

"And the tonic water is not a good sign," Alison added. "Have you ever noticed, Kitty, that when Sue doesn't have a glass of wine on Friday night it's because she really wants to drink a whole pitcher of martinis?"

Kit nodded. "I think she's applying the philosophy that if you feel you need a drink, you'd better not have it."

"Got it in one," Susannah said. "It's been a tough week."

"The museum project?" Kit sipped the glass of chardonnay which had materialized in front of her. "Better you than me. I don't know El Greco from van Gogh."

"Oh, that's an easy one," Alison said. "El Greco didn't paint flowers."

"I'll certainly remember to call you in if I need a consultant, Ali," Susannah muttered.

"I'll be happy to help out. Did you get the note I left in your in-basket about Universal Dynamics?"

"I saw it." Susannah sighed. "Ali, I know you wouldn't toss a new account to me if it wasn't my turn. But honestly, I've got so much to do right now that I'm not going to see daylight before the first of September. If one of you will take it over, I'll happily make it up to you later."

"You'd give up Universal Dynamics?" Kit stretched out a hand and laid it across Susannah's forehead. "You don't *feel* feverish, but—"

"I know. Being their PR firm would make Tryad known nationwide. I didn't say we shouldn't grab for the account, it's just that I don't have time right now. Would you rather I take on the job and do it badly?"

"It wouldn't be my first choice," Kit admitted.

"Exactly. So I'll swap you—either one of you. You handle Universal Dynamics, and I'll take over whatever annoying and time-consuming jobs you want to get rid of, just as soon as I get my head above water."

Ali was shaking her head. "It's not your turn, Sue."

Susannah frowned. "Then why did it land in my lap?"

"Remember the job you did for the conveyer belt people?"

"Kitty worked on that one, too," Susannah said warily.

"On the preliminaries," Kit said. "But you put the pieces together, presented it, and saved them from a whole rash of million-dollar lawsuits."

"So what's that got to do with Universal Dynamics? Do they make conveyer belts, too?"

"No," Alison said. "At least, I don't think so, though they seem to be involved in darned near everything else."

"And they give away millions of dollars every year," Kit added. "But the man who called—he's the vice president of public relations—wouldn't tell me exactly what he had in mind. He didn't want to talk to anybody but you about the specifics."

"Which brings us back to the original question. Why me?"

"Apparently somebody at Universal Dynamics knows somebody at Industrial Conveyer, and over coffee—"

"More likely it was Scotch and water," Kit offered.

"Whatever. You obviously came highly recommended."

Susannah groaned. "So tell this guy that my partners are every bit as competent, or they wouldn't be my partners."

"*You* tell him," Alison suggested. "I doubt he'd believe it, coming from Kit or me."

Kit nodded. "He'd probably think we were trying to scavenge your clients."

Susannah gave up. "All right. I'll call on Monday and fix it up. Which one of you wants the job?"

"I doubt you're going to persuade him to give anyone else a chance," Kit said. "And I can't possibly live up to your standards anyway, Sue, on what sounds like an *Alice in Wonderland* project. Thinking up three impossible things before breakfast is your department."

"Thanks a lot," Susannah said. "Ali?"

Alison frowned. "If you absolutely can't, I could probably muddle through. But you know how buried I am in this video production right now. And he did ask especially for you."

Susannah sighed and surrendered to the inevitable. "All right, I'll make time somehow. Does anybody have an aspirin?"

Both Kit and Alison fumbled in their purses, and a moment later two hands stretched out, a white tablet balanced on each palm.

"That's what I love best about you guys," Susannah said dryly as she scooped up both aspirins. "You're always right there when I need you, happy to help!"

Susannah was halfway to Rockford the following morning when her cellular phone rang, startling her so much she almost lost control of her car. She answered it warily, and Kit said, "Sorry to bother you. I'd forgotten till just this minute that it's your weekend to visit your mother.''

Susannah didn't comment. What was there left to say, after all, about her monthly visits? Instead, she said, ''If it's something critical, Kitty, I'll be back late tonight.''

''It's not. Not really. I just wanted to apologize for sounding heartless last night—as if I was trying to dodge my share of work.''

''What do you mean? I didn't think—''

''Come on, Sue, at least let me abase myself. You helped me out of a hole a couple of months ago. I haven't forgotten, and I didn't mean to sound ungrateful. But honestly, the guy at Universal Dynamics sounded as if it was you or nothing, that neither Alison nor I could get past the front door to work for him. What I should have said last night, though, is that if I can take over any of your other work to leave you free for whatever he wants—''

''You're still snowed under from your honeymoon, Kitty.''

''When you were also taking up the slack for me. I feel like a worm already, Sue, don't rub it in.'' But there was a smile in Kit's voice.

Susannah's heart warmed. The way all three of them looked out for each other was the cement which had created the partnership in the first place and had held it together in the first three difficult years. Now they were beginning to reap the results of all their hard work, but their consideration for each other was as deep as ever. Kit was the sensitive one—empathetic, understanding, and always taking everyone else's feelings into account before pondering her own. And though Alison could be nearly as gruff as a bear in winter, she was also—despite a bare two years' difference in their ages—something of a mother figure to the other two. She was the one who kept track of details, the one who made sure they all remembered to eat and sleep when deadlines loomed, the one who arranged celebrations for every step forward, no matter how minor.

Susannah knew she couldn't let them down. She'd managed incredibly difficult work schedules before, and if she was lucky, the man at Universal Dynamics would want something simple—something she could do in half a day and make Tryad look great.

But she wasn't going to count on it, any more than she was going to count on Marc Herrington falling off the face of the earth before Monday morning.

Elspeth Miller's home was on the outskirts of Rockford, so at least Susannah didn't have to fight her way through city traffic on that end of the journey. It was one of the blessings of her once-a-month trips. One of the few blessings.

The woman who greeted her at the front door was wearing street clothes, but no jewelry. Even her sturdy white shoes might not have identified her as a nurse to a stranger, but Susannah had known Karen Edgar for more than a year.

"How's your son doing at Yale?" Susannah asked, and only after the update was complete did she ask about her mother.

Karen said, "That's why I was waiting to see you. Physically, I think she's a little weaker. She tires more quickly, she gets frustrated more easily. And the periods of confusion are longer, and they're coming more often."

"If they get any more frequent," Susannah protested, "there won't be any time in between."

Karen nodded. "That's a possibility. It's very difficult to project the course of her illness, since no one knows quite why she's this way."

Only I know, Susannah thought.

"And in a way," Karen went on gently, "it might be

a blessing for her. She's so much happier when she thinks I'm the housekeeper instead of the director of nursing, and when she looks on the rest of the staff as her personal maids. Though I must say the janitor is having a difficult time of it. She keeps insisting that she will not stand for such a slovenly butler—"

"Oh, no."

"She's fired him a dozen times, and she can't understand why he keeps showing up for work."

"Maybe I should remind her how hard it is to find good help these days, and encourage her to give the poor guy another chance." But the humor in Susannah's tone didn't ring quite true. "Thanks for waiting to talk to me, Karen."

"I only wish it were better news."

Susannah shrugged. There would probably never be better news; she'd known that for several years, since Elspeth's gloomy moods and occasional tirades had clearly crossed the line between eccentricity and mental instability.

She walked slowly down the nursing home's long hall, past a cheerful recreation room where a couple of residents were playing backgammon and another was dozing in a wheelchair, past a row of sun-splashed bedrooms, to a private corner suite where Elspeth Miller was sitting at her desk, head bent over a box of stationery.

Susannah paused in the doorway, drew a deep breath, and forced a smile to her lips. "Hello, Mother."

Elspeth looked up, frowning as if she was puzzled. "Where have you been, Susannah? You said you'd help me with these invitations. They have to go in the mail today."

Susannah took the chair next to Elspeth's desk. "I've been at work, Mother."

"Young women of your social class shouldn't work.

If you'd only been sensible about marrying well, instead of insisting on that common laborer—''

"I didn't marry Marc. Remember?"

Elspeth's eyes took on a faraway look. "Oh?" For a moment she seemed to drift off even farther into a private world, and then her attention snapped back. "Well, it doesn't matter. If I'm going to hold this dinner party, I must let people know. You can write the invitations while I make out the seating chart. Start with the Marshes, and the Colemans, while I look through my diary and decide who else to invite."

Two hours later, Susannah kissed her mother's cheek and left Elspeth, worn out from planning a party which would never be, lying down for a rest. She stopped by the nurses' station and gave an aide the thick stack of envelopes and invitation cards—all engraved with Elspeth's full, formal name—which she had assembled under her mother's watchful direction. "Can you recycle these again, Beth?"

The aide tucked them into a drawer. "I'll wait till she's asleep," she promised, "and put them back in the box for next time."

Susannah's feet dragged down the long hall and across the parking lot to her car, and she sat behind the wheel for several minutes before she felt able to start the long drive back to Chicago.

How odd it was, she thought, that Elspeth had chosen today to mention Marc. It was the first time since her dementia had become severe that Susannah could remember her doing so. Had she somehow, in her single-mindedness, been able to read Susannah's thoughts?

Not that picking up the vibrations would be terribly difficult. With the earthquake Marc had set off in her life, it was a wonder Susannah was able to think of anything else at all.

*   *   *

Susannah called Pierce on Monday afternoon. The incredible silence had gone on long enough, she thought; it was time to find out whether the board had been amused, shocked, or titillated by Marc's announcement. Besides, she was close enough to being finished with the preliminary inventory that she had some questions. Should she proceed on her own, or simply turn the details over to Pierce so he could do the actual valuations?

The museum assistant who answered her call sounded breathless, and Pierce took longer than usual to come to the telephone. With the receiver cradled between shoulder and ear, Susannah opened her mail while she waited.

When Pierce finally picked up the call, his voice was cheery. "Susannah! I wasn't expecting to hear from you. Have a nice weekend, did you?"

She thought with a tinge of irony of her mother, and then realized that the question had an odd ring about it. Or perhaps it wasn't the question itself—which was surely innocuous—but Pierce's tone of voice which made it seem so strange.

"It was all right," she said cautiously. "Why?"

Pierce chuckled. "Because when you called, I was uncrating Cyrus's Evans Jackson canvas. It was delivered just this morning, with Herrington's best wishes."

One painting at a time, Marc had said. *Whenever Susannah sleeps with me...*

So when Marc handed over the Evans Jackson, of course Pierce had drawn the inevitable conclusion. Anybody who'd been at the Dearborn on Thursday night would think precisely the same thing.

Susannah dropped the telephone and put her head down on her desk blotter. So much for the notion that she could simply wait him out, until he finally realized that her refusal was firm. Marc had not only anticipated her, he'd raised the stakes.

CHAPTER SIX

PIERCE'S voice was faint and hollow. "Susannah? Are you still there?" He sounded anxious.

She reached out for the telephone she'd dropped. "I'm here."

"Now that we've got the Evans Jackson, we'll need to start thinking about how we're going to run the publicity campaign. This is a story that just begs to be—"

Susannah was horrified. "Pierce, you can't mean to tell everybody in Chicago that I'm sleeping with Marc Herrington!"

"I was talking about the acquisition itself, Susannah, not how we got the painting. Though I must say Herrington doesn't seem to think it's private information."

"Well, I think it's *very* private. And besides, I'm *not* sleeping with him."

"Whatever you say, Susannah." There was something just short of a chuckle in Pierce's voice. "The board thinks you're doing a tremendous job, by the way."

"You'll never make me believe they'd approve of something so—" Words failed her.

"Well, *approve* might be a little strong, though the women members seemed to think *they* wouldn't find any hardship in the deal. Oh, there was one exception—our accountant expressed a few reservations about how to put a figure on the donation. He said since Herrington's getting value in return, Internal Revenue might have some objections to crediting him with the full amount of—"

Susannah gasped. "There's no need to be crude," she

GET A FREE TEDDY BEAR...

You'll love this plush, cuddly Teddy Bear, an adorable accessory for your dressing table, bookcase or desk. Measuring 5 ½" tall, he's soft and brown and has a bright red ribbon around his neck – he's completely captivating! And he's yours *absolutely free*, when you accept this no-risk offer!

AND TWO FREE BOOKS!

Here's a chance to get **two free Harlequin Romance® novels** from the Harlequin Reader Service® **absolutely free!**

There's no catch. You're under no obligation to buy anything. We charge nothing – ZERO – for your first shipment. And you don't have to make any minimum number of purchases – not even one!

Find out for yourself why thousands of readers enjoy receiving books by mail from the Harlequin Reader Service. They like the **convenience of home delivery**…they like getting the best new novels months before they're available in bookstores…and they love our **discount prices!**

Try us and see! Return this card promptly. We'll send your free books and a free Teddy Bear, under the terms explained on the back. We hope you'll want to remain with the reader service – but the choice is always yours! (U-H-R 04/98)   **116 HDL CF67**

NAME

ADDRESS   APT.

CITY   STATE   ZIP

Offer not valid to current Harlequin Romance® subscribers. All orders subject to approval.

©1993 HARLEQUIN ENTERPRISES LIMITED   **Printed in U.S.A.**

NO OBLIGATION TO BUY!

snapped, and hung up on him. Pierce had a nerve to talk to her like that!

But annoyed as she was with Pierce, he was far from the main focus of her anger and frustration. It was past time she made herself clear to Marc. This kind of nonsense simply could not go on any longer.

She seized her car keys and stormed down the stairs.

As Susannah passed the arched doorway to the receptionist's office on her way to the back door and her car, Rita put the telephone down, half rose from her desk, and held up a hand. "Susannah—"

Susannah shook her head. "No time," she said over her shoulder. "I'm not sure when I'll be back. And if you get a collect call from the Cook County Jail, accept it. It'll be me, needing bail money on a murder charge!"

Too late, she realized that Rita wasn't alone in her office; sitting in one of the leather visitor's chairs was a man Susannah had never seen before. However, one quick glance was enough to tell her he was most likely a client; his brown hair was precisely cut, and his suit had *corporate middle management* written all over it. And he looked absolutely thunderstruck.

She sent a rueful smile his way and muttered, "Sorry. You know how these things go." Then, as fast as she could move without actually running, she retreated toward the back door.

Maybe, if she was lucky, he hadn't caught her name. Maybe, even if he had, he'd think she was only an employee. Maybe, even if he figured out who she was, he wouldn't think her gaffe important enough to mention to Alison or Kit—whichever one he was waiting to see. Maybe, even if he realized she was a partner, he wouldn't allow her comment to affect his opinion of Tryad....

Maybe.

But if he did—well, that was just one more black

mark to chalk up against Marc Herrington's account. One more, in a long, long series.

Susannah had cooled off somewhat by the time she reached the western suburbs; there was nothing like expressway traffic to redirect one's frustration. But as she came up the front walk to Cyrus's house, the sight of Marc, sprawled full-length in a patch of sunlit grass with O'Leary's head resting worshipfully on his outflung hand, inflamed her all over again. She would have slammed the gate, if the hydraulic hinge had allowed it. Since it didn't, she settled for storming across the lawn to stand over him, tapping her toes on the grass.

He looked about nine feet long, stretched out on the carpet of soft green, wearing jeans that were the most faded she'd seen yet. He couldn't have bought *them* from the Salvation Army, she thought; even a thrift store would have been reluctant to give shelf room to something so worn. His chest was bare; a pale blue shirt fluttered from its makeshift hook on a branch nearby.

"I suppose you've got some sort of excuse!" she exploded.

Marc slowly opened his eyes. "Any reason you're entitled to one?" he countered.

"Of course I'm entitled. It involves me."

He sat up and flexed his muscles. "Mowing the lawn involves you? I just finished, so I decided to take a break before I went in for a shower. If that bothers you, Susannah—"

O'Leary grumbled low in his throat about being disturbed, and shifted just far enough to put his chin on Marc's knee.

Now that she looked more closely, Susannah could detect on Marc's bare chest the last drops of drying sweat. His hair was mussed, and a few grass clippings clung to his skin, to his jeans, to his hair. The healthy

male animal, she thought, resting after his exertions...
Not that his effort cut any ice with her.

"Cyrus didn't have a lawn service?" she asked tartly.

"Sure he did. I need the exercise."

"Besides, why pay them when you can keep a few
more of Cyrus's dollars in your own pocket, right? Marc,
you know perfectly well why I'm here, and it's got nothing to do with grass. How dare you send that painting
down to the Dearborn?"

"Oh. That." He stretched, dislodging O'Leary again,
and sat up. "It's mine. I can do whatever I like with it."

"Unfortunately, Pierce and the Dearborn's board
seem to have forgotten that fact. All they remember is
that stupid so-called deal of yours, and they think....they
think I—" Her voice cracked.

"They think we spent the weekend together?" He almost sounded sympathetic. Susannah wanted to kick
him. "Sorry, darling, but that's really not *my* problem."

"And I suppose you didn't intend for them to draw
that conclusion? Come on, Marc. After what you said
Thursday night, sending that painting to the museum was
just like putting up a billboard on the Kennedy
Expressway saying *Susannah Miller slept with me!*"

Marc looked up at her admiringly. "What an idea! I
take back everything I ever said about public relations,
Susannah. It's a delightful field, and you're a natural. A
billboard—I'll have to look into that. Or would the sides
of city buses be even better? Since they're mobile, I'd
think more people would see—"

She cut him off. "Dammit, Marc, what's next? If you
start sending Pierce a painting a day—"

"Oh, no. I wouldn't even consider that." He pulled
himself to his feet and began dusting flecks of grass off
his jeans.

His tone, she thought, was just a little too innocent.
"Why not?"

"Would you make up your mind, Susannah? First you don't want me to make a daily donation, and now you sound suspicious because I've said I won't."

"You're not answering my question."

"It's elementary economics, my dear." He retrieved his shirt from the branch. "Cyrus didn't leave me an inexhaustible supply of paintings, and if I give them away without getting anything in return, it's hardly a good bargain from my point of view." He put on his shirt and began to button it.

Susannah couldn't help watching the process. He'd started at the bottom, and his fingers seemed to caress each button in turn. He stopped halfway up, leaving a good portion of chest still visible, and turned his attention to the sleeves, folding his cuffs up almost to the elbow.

How perfectly ridiculous, Susannah told herself. It was *undressing* which was supposed to be sexy. There was no reason at all for her mouth to go dry over a hint of chest and a pair of strong brown wrists when a few minutes ago she'd seen the whole works.

"Unless, of course," Marc added easily, "you plan to make it worth the sacrifice. In that case, I'll happily start crating up canvases—"

"Don't hold your breath. And you've just contradicted yourself about the Evans Jackson. If you don't believe in giving up something for nothing—"

"I consider it sort of a down payment."

Susannah sputtered. "On *me?*"

"Not exactly. You know how sometimes you have to put down earnest money to prove you're sincere about making a deal and you're not just negotiating for the fun of it? It's that sort of thing. And since that canvas seems to be your pal Pierce's favorite, it struck me as the perfect way to show that I mean to stand by my word all the way."

Susannah wanted to scream. "And, of course, since you hate the Evans Jackson anyway..."

"That factor did enter into my choice," Marc admitted. "If I'd had to look at it one more day I might have used it to carpet O'Leary's doghouse."

"You mean he isn't sleeping on your bed?" she snapped, and realized an instant too late what an opening she'd given him.

Marc smiled, a slow, warm, rich smile full of promise. "Oh, no." His voice was as sensual as the stroking of a feather against her skin. "That spot's reserved for you."

"I do *not* sleep with married men!"

The instant's silence seemed to drag out forever before Marc said, "There must be a reason for that vehemence. Is that why you didn't marry the father of your child, instead of honoring me with the title? Because he was already married?"

"I wish you would realize that incident has nothing to do with you!"

"Then why did you drag me into it?" he asked reasonably. "But you're right, it's only idle curiosity that makes me ask now. In any case, your objection doesn't apply."

"What?" Distracted by the tangent he'd taken, Susannah couldn't even remember for a moment where they'd started out.

"I'm not married. Whatever gave you the idea that I was?"

She could feel fury rising in her, fueled by his guileless tone. Fury—mixed with aggravation, a healthy dose of frustration, and a dash of...relief? *Surely not,* she told herself. She was just glad to finally have things straight, that was all.

"You did," she said tartly. "Remember? You said something about your marriage having gone sour anyway and how the mortgage and job hardly mattered any-more because Cyrus had so much money, so you didn't have any reason to go home.''

"Oh, that." He sounded almost apologetic. "I was speaking hypothetically. You looked so disappointed when you didn't see a wedding ring that I thought it might make you feel better to think I was miserable. And as for the bit about Cyrus's money—well, you seemed to expect that, too. Not that it isn't true enough, but—''

"Oh, fine," Susannah snapped. "Put the blame on me. I suppose next you're going to tell me the paintings-for-favors deal was my idea, too!''

The sarcasm in her tone was heavy enough to sink the average cabin cruiser, but it seemed to slide off Marc like butter across a hot skillet.

"But my darling," he said. "It was.''

She stared at him for the better part of a minute, while the soft green lawn seemed to undulate under her feet like Lake Michigan in a brisk summer breeze. Marc found a stick to throw for O'Leary, and he'd tossed it three times before Susannah found her voice.

"And just how did you twist that around?" she asked.

Marc shrugged. "You said something about it being important to protect myself.''

Susannah remembered the incident, vaguely. She'd been talking about looking out for his inheritance, hadn't she? And she'd been speaking ironically then, too.

"Well, the longer I thought about it," Marc went on easily, "the more I realized that the advice was good where you were concerned, too.''

Susannah shook her head in confusion. He couldn't be *serious*, surely—no matter how solemn he sounded. "Sleeping together is your definition of protecting your-self from me?''

"It does sound a bit strange, doesn't it?''

"*A bit?* I'd say it's world-class.''

"Let me give you an example. How do you prevent yourself from catching a dreadful disease?"

"I don't see what that has to do with—"

"By getting a shot—right?—which exposes you to a small dose of the bacteria or virus so your immune system creates antibodies."

Susannah said slowly, "I'm the dreadful disease, and going to bed with me is supposed to immunize you?"

Marc was obviously pleased with her quick uptake. "I suppose any kind of regular contact would do the job eventually, but I thought that sleeping together would be the fastest—"

"I've heard some lines in my day, Herrington, but that one deserves a place in the Smithsonian Institution. No, on second thought, *you* deserve a place in an institution!"

"You don't think it's a good idea? It would work the other direction, too, you know."

"Immunizing *me* against *you?* As if I needed any help!"

She tried not to look back as she stamped across the lawn to her car, but she couldn't quite stop herself. When she peeked over her shoulder, however, Marc wasn't watching her. He'd picked up the stick again and thrown it for O'Leary to chase.

The two of them, she thought, looked as if they hadn't a care in the world.

When Susannah got back to the office, the first thing she did was to pop her head into Rita's office. The secretary looked a bit wary.

Susannah didn't blame her. "I'm sorry for that outburst," she said. "I hope the client didn't go screaming off down the street?"

"No," Rita said carefully. "Though I'm sure for a

moment he wanted to. Alison came up just then, so it was all right."

Susannah felt relief flood through her. "I'll look around to make sure there aren't any clients in the room before I explode next time. I promise, Rita."

"That would be good. As long as you're here—" She reached for a file on the corner of her desk.

"I'll come back in a minute, all right? I really want to clear things up with Alison first."

Rita said dryly, "She said she wanted to see you, too."

"Ouch," Susannah muttered. "Is she down in her office?"

"No, she and Kit are in the conference room. It's not a private session, though. She said to send you in."

Susannah faced the closed doors of the conference room with trepidation. It wasn't that she was expecting any kind of reprimand; no one of them had that sort of power over the others. But the idea that she had disappointed her partners, had made life and work more difficult for them, was worse than any sort of scolding could be. They'd all worked hard to build Tryad—but any one of them could tear it down with a single act of carelessness.

The pocket doors were eight feet tall and solid oak, but so perfectly balanced that they moved with the touch of a finger. Susannah slid one door aside and cautiously put her head in, ready to back out if the conference looked serious after all.

The video script Alison had been working on for weeks was spread across the long table, and Kit was standing atop one of the leather chairs in her stocking feet. Susannah thought she might be demonstrating how to get a particular shot—but she didn't quite want to ask.

She didn't think the door had made any noise at all,

but two heads turned abruptly toward her as if pulled by a single string.

"Sorry," she said. "I didn't mean to interrupt."

"We're almost finished," Alison said.

"And in any case, I can't possibly concentrate on mere video now that you're here." Kit jumped down from the chair. "Who on earth is it you've murdered, Sue? Pierce? Marc Herrington? Someone we've never heard of?"

Susannah sighed. "Nobody at all."

"That's the way, dear," Kit said approvingly. "Deny it to your last breath. Did he or she deserve it? And are you going to get away with it, do you think—or will Ali and I have to take over all your work? If that's going to be a problem, maybe the three of us together can come up with an alibi—"

Susannah stuck her tongue out at Kit and turned to Alison. "Look, I'm really sorry. Rita says I upset your client, and—"

Alison was shaking her head. "Not my client. I happened to walk through right after you made your announcement, but I've been working on the shooting script for the video all afternoon."

"He was yours then, Kitty?"

"Nope. I've been up in the production room most of the day."

"Then who..."

Rita spoke from the open doorway behind Susannah, her voice almost prim. "I tried to tell you before you came in here, Susannah. The gentleman was here to see you. I was trying to ring up to your office when you came storming down."

Susannah closed her eyes in pain, and opened them again a second later. "Wait a minute. I didn't have an appointment this afternoon, did I? I certainly wouldn't have forgotten a client, especially a new…'' Her voice trailed off.

''He left his card,'' Rita said, and held it out.

Susannah took the pale ivory rectangle with the same enthusiasm she'd have displayed for a hot ember dropped in her hand. *I was right,* she thought as she scanned the fine block letters which spelled out his name. *I've never met this guy before. Never heard of him, in fact…*

Except, she realized, that last wasn't quite true. She had heard of Amos Richards, not by name but by title.

She sank into the closest chair and looked at the card again, hoping the type might by some magic have changed. But it was still the same.

Amos Richards, vice president of public relations, Universal Dynamics.

Universal Dynamics, the new client who had asked especially for Susannah. The new client whose public relations budget would probably make every other account they'd ever dreamed of look like petty cash.

The new client who could make Tryad a household name, good or bad, across the nation. All Amos Richards had to do was tell his story…

And—thanks to Marc Herrington—what a story she had given him to tell!

Susannah didn't realize she was listening for Kit's footsteps on the stairs until she found herself following her partner down the hall to the front office. She put her head in the door just as Kit was sitting down at her desk, and asked, ''Mind if I come in for a minute before you get involved in a project?''

Kit pushed her chair back. ''If it's Universal Dynamics that's bothering you, Sue—''

''It is,'' Susannah said frankly. She flung herself on Kit's chaise longue wrong-end-to and propped her feet on the raised headrest. "I blew it, and now I don't have any idea how to proceed. Let the whole thing cool off for a couple of days, and hope in the meantime he'll see the humor in it? Or will waiting only make me look careless and unprofessional?"

"Heavens, I don't know. Do you want a coin to flip? Sue, stop beating yourself up. It could have been any of us."

"Not Alison," Susannah said drearily. "Ali's incapable of embarrassing Tryad."

"Oh, I don't know. There are certain depths to Ali…"

"Of course there are, but they're all *good* ones! While I—"

"Don't waste time feeling sorry for yourself, Sue. It's not like you. Remember who was the black sheep around here a couple of months ago?"

"You—but at least you had a good excuse. You were in love."

Kit didn't answer, and after a while Susannah stopped staring at the ceiling and peered at her. The expression on Kit's face was soft, amused—almost maternal.

Susannah sat up so fast she felt dizzy. "Now wait a minute," she protested. "If you're jumping to conclusions about *me*—"

"I wasn't, actually. I was wondering what might happen when Ali falls in love."

Susannah sank back on the chaise. "She won't. If Alison ever decides to get married, she'll run an ad in the classifieds under *Help Wanted*."

Kit smiled. "You may be right. Anyway, as long as we're talking about wanting help, here's my advice. Call Amos Richards and get it over with."

"Don't you think it might be better to wait?"

"For what? So you can have another couple of days to stew about it?" Kit turned back to her desk. "Now get out of here, I've got work to do. And so do you."

Susannah picked herself up off the chaise and gave Kit an impulsive hug. "You do have a way of putting things, darling."

Her heart was lighter as she returned to her own office, and Amos Richards's card, propped up against the base of her desk lamp, no longer looked as threatening. That was one of the great things about having partners—and especially these partners. They were far too caring, far too precious, to let down. She couldn't do anything less than her best where Universal Dynamics was concerned...or in regard to Cyrus Albrecht's art collection, either.

But if Marc remained obstinate...just how much of a sacrifice *would* she make, for Tryad's sake?

"Oh, now there's a cheery thought," she muttered and reached for the phone. The best reason she could think of for calling Amos Richards was that it would keep her from thinking about Marc for a few minutes. Marc, and that incredible suggestion of his that physical attraction was some sort of virus and sleeping together would keep the infection from getting worse.

Getting worse. He hadn't exactly phrased it that way, but the implication had been clear. And now that she thought about it...

Susannah sat with the phone in her hand, considering the implications, for a long time. And then she began to smile.

Susannah wasn't at all surprised, as the afternoon drew toward a close, when Rita phoned upstairs to tell her that Marc had dropped in. "He said to tell you he'd be out front playing baseball whenever you got through. And something about if you sneaked out the back, he knows where you live."

"Well, if he comes in for something else, tell him I wouldn't dream of trying to avoid him and I'll be down as soon as I can. That might keep him out of everybody's hair for a while."

She took her time, though, straightening up her office, filing every last paper on her desk and making out tomorrow's to-do list, before she picked up her briefcase and started down the stairs.

The impromptu baseball game had ended, and Marc was sitting on Tryad's front porch steps. He'd changed into a slightly less-disreputable pair of jeans and a pullover shirt, and he was chewing on a stalk of grass and staring at the tiny park across the street.

Susannah sat down beside him. "Poor baby," she crooned. "You just can't stay away from me, can you?"

A gleam sprang to life in his dark eyes. "It's terrible," he agreed. "I can feel the virus starting to take hold."

"But that's not it. You've been carrying a torch for me for eight years."

"You know," Marc said with a note of discovery in his voice. "I believe you're right. Now that I stop to think about it, I realize that I've compared every woman in my life to you. Though I don't suppose there have been more than three hundred of them in the last eight years, so perhaps that's really not a fair sample."

"Three hundred?"

"Give or take."

"That's a new woman every ten days, Marc."

"Is it, really? I never took time to actually figure it out."

"Never *had* time, more likely," Susannah muttered. "However, it only helps to illustrate the point—"

"I thought you must have one somewhere."

"That you're wrong, Marc. Sleeping with me won't immunize you. It's too late for that. You'll only want me more."

His arm slid easily around her shoulders and drew her

tightly against his side. "So let's try it and find out who's right—shall we?"

"Oh, no. I can't allow you to take such a chance. If you were to run out of paintings, you see—"

He obviously wasn't listening. His other hand came up under Susannah's chin, firmly raising her face to his. The arm around her shoulders seemed to harden into steel, and his gaze focused on her lips. The pressure of his mouth against hers was gentle, and yet the effect on Susannah was ravishing. Suddenly none of her muscles would work right. She raised a hand to push him away, but her fingers clutched at his collar instead, holding her closer to him. He eased her back till she was almost lying on the porch floor, and her hands slid to the back of his neck to support herself. The brick step was chilly, she told herself, but deep inside she knew that she wasn't seeking to avoid the cold, but to cling to his warmth...

Kit's voice sounded as if she were a long way away. "Don't mind us."

Susannah fought to open her eyes and looked up into two interested faces. Not only Kit but Alison stood over them.

Susannah winced.

"Ali and I do hate to be troublesome," Kit went on. "But... Oh, I've got it. How about if we just go out the back door and walk around the block rather than make you move? No, really—it's no trouble at all."

A rusty-sounding voice from the porch next door, the twin of Tryad's, said, "What's going on over there?" A moment later, a wrinkled face appeared above the low dividing wall.

It was the first time in nearly two months that any of them had seen Mrs. Holcomb outside. *And I believed things couldn't get worse,* Susannah thought.

Mrs. Holcomb stared at the tableau for a long moment. "Right on the porch. Well, I never!"

Alison said, under her breath, "I wouldn't doubt *that* in the least."

Kit elbowed her and raised her voice. "It's all right, Mrs. Holcomb. We have everything under control."

Marc grinned. Carefully, he arranged Susannah against the porch pillar; if she'd been able to move she'd have been furious with him for treating her like a china doll. He stood up and offered his hand to Kit and then to Alison. "My pleasure."

"Oh, we could guess that much," Kit murmured. "You must be Marc Herrington. Nice to meet you. Perhaps another time—when Sue's feeling up to it—we can all sit down for a chat."

She stepped over Susannah's feet and sauntered off down the walk without looking back. Alison paused, looking down at Susannah with a troubled frown.

"It's all right, Ali," she muttered.

Alison's frown didn't disappear. She surveyed Marc for a full minute, but whatever she saw seemed to reassure her. "See you tomorrow, Sue," she said finally, and followed Kit.

"Nice people you work with." Marc sat down on the top step. "Refresh my memory. *Who* was it you said wouldn't be able to handle the aftereffects of sleeping together?"

Susannah considered banging her head against the porch pillar a few dozen times.

"It's a good thing I talked to Pierce this afternoon," Marc went on, "and asked which of Cyrus's paintings he'd like next. Shall I call him back and tell him to expect another shipment tomorrow?"

CHAPTER SEVEN

SUSANNAH pulled herself to her feet. "If you think for one minute that I'm going to stick around for any more of this conversation—"

Marc bounded up. "But, Susannah, darling, I came all the way over here to ask you a question, and I haven't had a chance."

"You've had all kinds of chances. You've just wasted them on other things."

"A couple of questions, actually. First...but before I ask, do you suppose we could go somewhere a little more private? Unless you like having the neighbors listen in. I don't, myself."

"Funny. I wouldn't have thought that sort of thing would bother you," Susannah said dryly. "And no, I don't want to go somewhere more private and risk a repetition of that attack."

"Oh, I never repeat myself," Marc said earnestly. "But of course I understand if you're afraid to trust your self-control."

Susannah started to sputter.

"So how about coffee?"

"And if I don't agree, I suppose you'll just send Pierce another painting?"

"Susannah, my dear, you have such delightful ideas."

"You tempt me," she said. "You really do. If I can annoy you enough times..."

"I said Cyrus didn't leave me an infinite number of paintings—and that's the truth, he didn't. But did you know he had a warehouse?"

"You're joking."

Marc smiled. "Try me. We could go there, if you'd like. It's private, and we could stop at a deli for coffee to go."

"Thanks, anyway."

"Tomorrow, then. We'll have to inventory it sometime."

The mere thought was enough to make Susannah dizzy. A whole warehouse full of paintings? "Not tomorrow. I have to go over to the museum in the morning to talk to Pierce about publicity——" She caught herself too late, but tried to smooth over the mistake. "And I have to do some research, too. I've got an appointment with a very important new client."

Marc didn't take the bait and ask about the client, as Susannah had hoped he would. Not that she'd have told him—or anyone else outside Tryad—about Amos Richards and Universal Dynamics. Only when there was a signed contract would she so much as breathe the name. And that was still a long way off; she hadn't even talked to the man himself yesterday when she'd called to make the appointment, only to his secretary. Far too many things could still go wrong to be making any announcements.

Marc rubbed his knuckles along his jaw. "I'll bet that awkward hesitation means you and Pierce will be talking about the Evans Jackson," he mused. "Isn't it odd he forgot to mention the matter of publicity to me? I'd think the donor would be an important part of any announcement."

Susannah thought Pierce's silence hadn't been an oversight; it was pure good sense. But there was no point in admitting any more than she had to. "It's not odd at all. Most donors want to maintain their privacy."

"And miss all the fun?"

"Even with anonymous donations, there's still the pure satisfaction of giving," Susannah said dryly.

"Which is a frame of mind I'm sure you'll never experience."

"Probably not. Why settle for one sort of thrill when you can have several?"

"There are good reasons for wanting privacy, you know. It's not exactly pleasant being hounded by every museum director who thinks you might be persuaded to give him something, too. Keeping donors' names private protects them."

"Somehow," Marc said thoughtfully, "I doubt that's an entirely philanthropic move. It also protects the museum from competition, doesn't it?"

Susannah ignored him. "And there have been cases where a collector made a donation, got a lot of public notice, and was later the target of theft. That happened several years ago in upstate New York. A whole collection gone, and it's never been traced."

"Gone," Marc mused. "At least that way, I wouldn't have to fuss over the damned things anymore. And I could probably even deduct the loss on my taxes, right? Which brings me to another question...." He paused. "Are we going to have dinner, or not?"

"Dinner? I thought the invitation was for coffee."

"The longer you put off answering, the higher the stakes get."

"And it doesn't take any great intellectual development to figure out what's next on your escalating scale. All right, come in, and I'll make coffee." Susannah pushed open the front door and led the way through the brownstone's front hall and down the stairs, past Alison's always-neat office to the kitchen. "Regular or flavored? We've got Irish cream and hazelnut."

"Regular. I never did understand the attraction of the fancy stuff. When I drink coffee, I want to taste coffee... Do I have to dial anything special to use this phone?"

Susannah looked over her shoulder. "No. Why?"

Marc was rustling the pages of the telephone directory. "I'm ordering the food. Do you still like Chinese as well as you used to, or would you prefer pizza?"

"I'd prefer..." Susannah decided it was a lost cause; the longer she argued, the longer he'd hang around. "Chinese is fine. There's a place a couple of blocks down the street that delivers. The number's scribbled on the cover of the phone book."

She turned on the coffeepot and put two cups on the plain square pine table in the center of the room. The chairs grouped around it were straight-backed and notoriously uncomfortable; the set had been Alison's choice, and Kit and Susannah had teased her ever since about her tactful way of keeping coffee breaks to a minimum.

Now, it seemed like a good idea. No matter how much of a nuisance Marc wanted to be, he couldn't ignore the kink in his spine which one of those chairs was bound to produce.

She listened as he placed an order—for enough food to feed an entire boarding school, in Susannah's opinion. She hoped he wasn't planning to stay long enough to eat every bite of it.

He pulled out a chair and propped an elbow on the table. "About the question of taxes," he said.

"Is that what we were talking about?"

"Had you forgotten already, in the fascination of my presence? It has come to my attention that it might be more advantageous for me to donate Cyrus's paintings to a national museum instead of a local one."

"Why?" The coffeepot gave an arthritic creak as it finished brewing, and Susannah crossed the kitchen to fill the cups.

"Joe Brewster says the tax advantages would be better. But I thought I should ask your opinion."

"Me? I'm no tax expert."

"Did I say you were?"

"Oh, I see. You expect me to try to talk you out of it. And if I do, you'll jump to the conclusion it's because I really want to sleep with you after all."

"Don't you, sweetheart?"

Susannah set a steaming cup in front of him. She had to exert great willpower to keep from tipping the contents over his head. "No. And don't let me keep you from doing whatever your attorney thinks will be the best deal financially."

Marc grinned. "And I'm sure you'll enjoy hearing me tell Pierce and the board why they're not getting the rest of the collection." He took a long swallow of his coffee and sat back, cradling the cup in his palm.

"It can't be any worse than the tasteless joke you've been carrying out all along." She only wished she believed that.

"I just thought it was fair to warn you, that's all."

"Well, thanks for the consideration. I'll brace myself. If that's all you wanted to tell me, Marc, there's no need to wait around for the food. I'll call and cancel the order, and—"

To Susannah's utter amazement, he drained his coffee cup in a gulp, set it down on the table, and stood up. "All right. See you—well, I'm not sure when, since you'll be busy all day tomorrow. Let me know when you want to start inventorying the warehouse."

Before she could gather her thoughts, Marc's footsteps resounded from the stairs and through the empty halls. The front door banged, and the brownstone fell utterly silent.

It shouldn't have been so easy, Susannah thought. She'd almost forgotten; hadn't he said he had a couple of questions? So what was the other one—the one he hadn't asked? And why had he changed his mind? Why had he walked out instead?

There had to be a reason he'd left her there, sitting over a rapidly cooling cup of coffee, wondering why he'd gone—and wondering, too, why she wasn't simply glad to be alone.

Pierce was in the new acquisitions gallery when Susannah reached the Dearborn late the following morning. He was showing off the Evans Jackson canvas, now hanging on the most prominent wall of the entire museum, to a couple of elderly matrons who looked more puzzled than impressed.

Behind the matrons' backs, he waggled a warning hand at Susannah, and she obediently retreated to his office to flip through a stack of art magazines and wait impatiently for tour's end.

She was already on her third magazine when she saw the glossy full-page ad for Universal Dynamics's latest philanthropic project, a new ballet the company had commissioned. It was lucky she'd spotted it at all, at the speed she'd been turning pages. But the ad was an eye-catcher, done by one of the best agencies in Chicago. She studied it closely, and couldn't find a flaw with the layout, the copy, or the overall impression.

If she hadn't already been eager to meet with Amos Richards and to work with Universal Dynamics, that near-perfect ad would have changed her mind. Not only would having the company as a client be a feather in Tryad's cap, but for Tryad to be associated with an internationally known ad firm like the one which had done this campaign would be a giant step for the business, as well. The two fields of advertising and public relations walked hand in hand; each depended on the other. And if the two firms worked well together there might be no end of referrals and future business...

Susannah checked her pocket calendar. Yes, she'd remembered the time correctly—her appointment with

Amos Richards was at four o'clock, at Universal Dynamics's suburban headquarters.

Suddenly, that meeting had become even more important.

Pierce came into his office, dropped into his chair, and fanned himself with the closest magazine—the one Susannah had been reading. "I thought they'd never get finished yakking," he said. "How is the inventory of Cyrus's collection going?"

"Slowly. Did you know he had a warehouse, too?"

"Really?" The gleam in Pierce's eyes made him look almost predatory. "I always wondered what he did with the canvases he took down. He was always buying but never selling—and even that enormous house didn't have enough walls to hold everything he owned."

"I haven't seen the warehouse yet," Susannah warned.

"Well, take your time over it. I don't figure there's any hurry about either the inventory or the valuations, since we're getting the collection bit by bit—"

Susannah cut in. "I don't think you should count on that."

"Why?"

"Because it sounds as if Marc's going to change his mind."

Before she could tell him about the tax question, Pierce said, "Do you expect me to believe you can't hold the attention of a man like Herrington for longer than a weekend? Come on, Susannah—"

Marc said, from the doorway, "Oh, she can hold my attention—if she wants to badly enough." His voice held a sensual throb.

I should have known he wouldn't forget I was coming here this morning, Susannah thought. "I wish you'd make up your mind, Herrington. Yesterday you tell me you're going to give the whole works to some national organization, but now—''

"What?" Pierce's eyes almost popped.

"Only if you don't follow all the way through with the original terms," Marc said. He came to stand behind her chair, his hands warm on the muscles at the back of her neck in the casual, sure touch of a lover. "Didn't I make myself clear? I'd never take that option away from you, darling. Believe me."

"You know perfectly well I'm not going to—''

Pierce sagged back in his chair. "Oh. That's all right, then. I thought I was doomed to have a heart attack just as the television cameras arrived."

For a moment, Susannah wasn't sure she'd heard correctly. "Television? You mean right now?"

Pierce wouldn't look directly at her. "I probably shouldn't have mentioned..." An accusing note crept into his voice. "You caught me by surprise with that crack about another museum, Susannah, or I wouldn't have said anything about it."

"Oh, really?" Susannah said dryly. "And when, exactly, were you going to bring it up? Or am I supposed to read your mind? You hired me to take care of publicity, Pierce, but if I'm going to be responsible for the results I'd certainly like to know what's going on."

He shot a sideways, sneaky glance at Marc. "Can we talk about this later?"

"You mean after the cameras have come and gone? No. I thought our discussion this morning was about what publicity we were going to seek, and how to go about getting it. I haven't even thought through a coordinated campaign yet, much less worked out the details, but you've already arranged for television coverage? What were you thinking of, Pierce?"

"Well, you've been pretty busy for the last few

days,'' Pierce pointed out. ''And this was important, so of course I called the stations myself.''

''What's so momentous that you couldn't phone me before you called in the media?''

Pierce darted another look at Marc and dropped his voice. ''I'd rather not say, Susannah.''

Marc came around Susannah's chair and planted himself on the corner of Pierce's desk. ''Oh, come on,'' he urged. ''I already know this conference is about my Evans Jackson, because Susannah let that much slip out last night.''

''You don't need to make it sound like pillow talk,'' Susannah muttered.

''Why not?'' From his commanding position on the desk, Marc looked down at Pierce. ''Don't you think it's a little rude not to let me know what's going on?''

Pierce looked at the ceiling. His words almost ran together; he sounded like a child confessing that he'd robbed the cookie jar. ''I found out late yesterday that Evans Jackson himself is going to be in town today.''

Susannah sagged in her chair. Pierce was right; the reuniting of artist and canvas in the painting's new home was too good an opportunity to miss. And though he should have consulted her, the point was hardly one she could argue. If she'd been in his shoes, she'd have done the same thing.

And, she reflected, she wouldn't have wanted to talk about it in front of Marc, either. If he were to tell the celebrated artist that it had been a difficult choice between handing the canvas over to the Dearborn or using it as carpet for the doghouse... That alone would be bad enough, but if the television crew happened to be standing by when he said it, the Dearborn would make the network news.

''Besides,'' Pierce muttered, ''I didn't want to disturb

you last night, Susannah—in case you were doing something really important.''

Every scrap of sympathy Susannah had been feeling for Pierce's difficult position vanished with a puff at the sly note in his voice. *Before this is over,* she thought, *I will probably run Pierce through the office shredder. Twice.*

From the corner of her eye, she saw Marc trying in vain to suppress a smile. *And Marc, too,* she added. Though, on the other hand, the shredder was too good a finish for him. She'd have to think of something worse.

"But the TV crew won't be here for a while," Pierce went on. "So if there's something I can do for you in the meantime, Mr. Herrington, before you have to go—''

Marc's eyebrows rose. "Go? Oh, I wouldn't dream of leaving. And besides, I thought you said you were afraid you'd still be having a heart attack when they arrived—which surely means the wait won't be long.''

Pierce looked disgruntled.

"What a thrill it will be," Marc mused, "to actually meet Evans Jackson, and hear his explanation of that incredible work…''

"But you hate…I mean," Pierce stammered, "you don't want to be involved at this stage. The notoriety it would cause…the invasion of your privacy—''

"I've already told him he'll have museums and fund-raisers from all over the country annoying him if he goes public," Susannah said. "He seemed to think that would be an advantage—but he was probably only being contrary. So if you tell him you *want* him to be involved, Pierce, perhaps he'll run for cover.''

Marc shook his head sadly. "What kind of public relations person are you, Susannah, not to take full advantage of free television time? Let's see—what can I do to be sure this bit of videotape will bring the museum the maximum amount of attention?''

Pierce's face was taking on an alarming resemblance to an avocado, Susannah noticed. Of course, she was probably turning a little green with apprehension, herself.

Susannah's nerves were still jangling when she got back to Tryad at midafternoon. It wasn't that Marc had done or said anything particularly awful; he'd actually behaved rather well. If, of course, she disregarded the occasional remark in which only her already-tuned antennae found hidden meaning—as when he'd told Evans Jackson, with a perfectly straight face and directly in front of the camera, that he was proud to be known as a *former* owner of his work.

The artist, on a particularly egotistical high, had taken the remark as a compliment and launched into a description of himself as the next—and ultimate—Picasso. Afraid that Marc's self-restraint had reached the expiration point, Susannah could do nothing but watch as he opened his mouth to respond. Then, as if he could hear the wordless plea which echoed through her brain, Marc glanced over at her, and smiled.

Why she should have found that reassuring, Susannah didn't quite know; he'd smiled at her before and an instant later gone straight on with whatever stunning announcement or devastating question or suggestive statement he'd intended to make all along. But somehow this smile was different, and she felt her tension draining away.

She'd sagged against the wall and closed her eyes in relief, and when she opened them again a moment later, she was startled to find Marc watching her, his head tipped a little to one side as if he was puzzled.

Her heart had started to pound—she thought it was with fear of what he might do next. But in the next split second, Marc turned his head and murmured something to Evans Jackson that—astonishingly—sounded like agreement. And Susannah was left wondering if she'd actually seen that look of perplexity or only imagined it.

Despite the surface amicability, however, Susannah didn't dare leave the museum until the television crew was safely out of the way. She couldn't prevent trouble, but she might be able to engineer damage control. Once the cameras were gone, however, keeping the peace wasn't her responsibility anymore. If Marc told Evans Jackson what he really thought of the Dearborn's new acquisition, at least the moment wouldn't be preserved for the ages on videotape.

The packing-up process seemed to take forever. As the camera truck pulled away, Pierce—in a sudden and unusually expansive mood—threw an arm around Evans Jackson's shoulders and said, "Let's all have lunch to celebrate."

Marc looked stunned. Susannah smothered a smile, then glanced at her watch and was horrified. She had less than two hours till her appointment with Amos Richards, and the portfolio she'd prepared for him to show the quality of Tryad's work was still lying on her desk blotter back at the office, minus the finishing touches.

She made her excuses and rushed out to her car, wishing that she'd had a couple of minutes to spare to see whether the lunch date really happened. Had Pierce honestly meant to invite Marc, or had he stumbled accidentally into the invitation? Would he follow through, or make an excuse to cancel?

She parked her car illegally beside the fire hydrant directly in front of the brownstone and made a detour downstairs to the kitchen. Even though she didn't really have time for lunch, she knew better than to make an important presentation on an empty stomach.

Kit was leaning into the refrigerator, fumbling through

bags and boxes. "I'd have sworn I left a Coke in here yesterday," she muttered as Susannah came in. "Maybe it's hiding behind... What's all this stuff doing here, anyway? Mo shu pork, egg foo yung, wontons, sweet and sour chicken, crab rangoon, pot-stickers... Are we representing a new restaurant, or the entire Chinese government?"

Susannah sighed. "Neither. It's just leftovers." She was darned if she'd admit that she'd sat over her coffee last night till the delivery man pounded on the front door, completely forgetting that she'd intended to call the restaurant and cancel Marc's order. Left without options, she'd paid the bill and—unable to face so much as a bite of Chinese food just then—shoved the boxes and bags helter-skelter into the refrigerator.

No, she wasn't going to confess what had happened; she'd only give Kit an excuse for finding hidden meanings in Susannah's preoccupation.

Kit stopped rummaging and looked thoughtful. "Well, if this is the leftovers, I wish I'd been invited to the party."

Susannah reached for a fork and the carton of crab rangoon. "No, you don't. Believe me, you've got the best of it right here." She didn't look back, but she knew Kit was watching her, and frowning, as she left the room.

She'd have liked to spend another hour polishing up her presentation, but fighting traffic was going to take most of the time she had left. She threw her samples into a big leather portfolio, gathered up her handbag and the crab rangoon, smoothed a hand over her hair, and headed back downstairs. It wouldn't be the first time she'd eaten lunch at a series of traffic lights.

At the curb, Marc was just getting out of Cyrus's Cadillac, which he'd parked in the legal space just behind Susannah's car. He waved a hand at the fireplug. "You know, you could get a ticket, doing that."

Susannah sighed. "We aren't all incredibly lucky enough to find a space just when we need it." She eyed the box of chocolates he'd tucked under his arm and said, "For me? Let me guess. I know you're soothing a guilty conscience, but I can't quite figure out whether it's over the way you acted this morning—"

"The way I acted?" Marc sounded hurt. "I was a perfect gentleman. Not once did I burst out laughing."

"—Or the fact that you stuck me with the tab for the food last night."

"Well, I'm certainly not feeling guilty about that. You said you'd cancel it. What happened, Susannah? Was there something else on your mind which made you forget?"

That jab struck a little too close to the bone for comfort, Susannah thought. Well, she'd asked for it. "You certainly owe me one."

"Dinner, you mean? Oh, I'll happily pay that debt. Tonight, seven o'clock." It was not a question. "I'll pick you up."

"I was talking about the candy, not dinner."

Marc shook his head. "Sorry, but you can't have the candy. It's for your neighbor, to make up for the shock we gave her. The trouble is, I can't remember her name. I know it was mentioned yesterday, but I…" He cleared his throat. "I had other things on my mind at the time."

"You brought chocolates for Mrs. Holcomb? You might as well eat them yourself, because you'll never get past the door."

"Even with an abject apology?"

"She won't let the meter readers in, much less charming strangers bearing candy."

"Thanks, honey. It's nice to know you find me charming."

Susannah tried to ignore him. "She'll probably call the police and tell them you're trying to poison her because of what she saw yesterday."

Marc rubbed his knuckles along his jaw. "Does a lack of faith run in this neighborhood? Though for a while today, over at the museum, I thought you were actually starting to trust me."

Confusion rippled through Susannah's mind. Was that what had happened—she'd actually trusted him not to embarrass her after all?

Surely not, she told herself. With all the stunts Marc had pulled over the last few days, she'd have to be an utter fool to trust him. And yet...

He'd smiled at her, and she'd relaxed—*before* he'd shown that he wasn't going to turn Evans Jackson into a laughingstock in front of the television cameras.

He raised a hand to her face and brushed the side of his index finger down her cheek. "I'm not such a bad guy, Susannah."

The streak of skin he'd touched tingled. She wanted to reach up and rub the sensation away. Or ask him to do so—except then the tingle would never vanish. It would grow and spread and take over...

"I—I have an appointment." Her voice was little more than a whisper.

"See you later, then." He started up the sidewalk to Mrs. Holcomb's door, whistling under his breath.

For a moment, Susannah stood absolutely still. He was referring to their supposed dinner engagement, she realized. She'd never actually turned it down. Well, she certainly didn't have time for an argument now.

She had to maneuver carefully to get her car free. She glanced back to make sure she was clearing the corner of Cyrus's Cadillac, and caught a glimpse of Marc on Mrs. Holcomb's front porch. The door was wide open, and Mrs. Holcomb stood in full view, beaming at him.

Susannah's jaw dropped. What on earth had the man said to make the recluse open her door?

In her astonishment, she forgot about the Cadillac until she felt a soft thud as the back of her car bumped into the front of Marc's.

He obviously heard the impact, for he turned and shook a gentle finger at her. A moment later he disappeared inside Mrs. Holcomb's house.

In the three years Tryad had occupied the brownstone, none of the partners had ever been invited to cross Mrs. Holcomb's threshold. And though all three of them tried to keep an eye on the house and its lonely occupant, if it wasn't for the ever-present flutter of the lace curtain at her front window, they wouldn't have known for certain whether she was still alive. Sometimes weeks went by with none of them actually catching a glimpse of her.

Now, in the space of twenty-four hours, Marc had not only lured the woman out onto her porch to supervise the neighborhood goings-on, but he'd actually gotten past that triple-locked door...

"It would be worth it to go to dinner with him," Susannah muttered, "just to hear about the inside of that house."

The thought created a surprising sort of glow deep inside her, a glow which couldn't be explained, no matter how hard she tried, by any amount of interest in Mrs. Holcomb's interior decorating.

As she drove across Chicago toward Universal Dynamics, the carton of crab rangoon forgotten on the seat beside her, Susannah wondered why the idea should be so inviting.

I thought you were actually starting to trust me, he'd said.

Was he right? Heaven knew she had no reason to trust. And yet, embarrassing though his stunts had been, nothing he'd done had actually been hurtful to her or anyone else.

Was it possible that the reason she'd been so startled last night, when he'd left her sitting in the kitchen, wasn't because she was suspicious of his sudden cooperation, but because she hadn't wanted him to leave?

And what would be so wrong about admitting that she might actually like to spend an evening with him? He was charming and funny and unpredictable. Once, she had been fond of him...

Perhaps she had even loved him? No, she told herself. She'd been too immature for that. Too immature, too rebellious, too foolish....

She wondered what would happen if, over dinner tonight, she simply told him what had really happened eight years ago. And then she ordered herself not to be ridiculous.

She had just ten minutes to spare before her appointment when she pulled into Universal Dynamics's parking lot, and most of that time was consumed in the walk through the sprawling building to Amos Richards's office. His secretary showed her directly in, and the man she remembered from her glimpse of him in Rita's office rose from behind a large desk to shake hands.

"It's good to finally meet you," he said, and gestured to the chair beside his desk. "Bring some coffee, please, Lisa."

Susannah balanced the portfolio across her knees and forced herself to smile. She could feel her throat muscles tightening, and only long practice kept her voice low and confident. "I'm glad to have the opportunity. I must apologize for my outburst the day you visited Tryad." What she wanted to ask, but didn't dare, was why he'd made that pilgrimage. Vice presidents of major corporations generally didn't go visiting; they summoned support people to come to them. Had he been checking out the looks of the place? Judging the caliber of Tryad's work by the atmosphere of the surroundings? Stranger things had happened. The important thing now was that she had one last chance to make a good impression.

The secretary brought in a coffee tray, and the business of pouring and sweetening consumed several minutes. Susannah sat back with her cup in hand and waited for the first of the questions which would determine whether this was the last meeting, or the first of many.

Instead, Amos Richards stirred his coffee and talked about the weather. With that exhausted, he asked about her preferences in cultural events. Did she care for opera? And what about ballet?

Maybe, Susannah thought, she'd been wrong even to hope. Maybe she had no chance at all, and this whole event was a waste of time. From the way Amos Richards was proceeding, he had no intention of getting down to business. He was going through the motions—no doubt so he could tell whoever had recommended Susannah, and Tryad, that he'd checked her out and found her unsuitable for his needs.

She was annoyed at him for not giving her a second chance, but even more so at herself for having—however innocently—blown the first one. And, with nothing to lose, she set her cup aside and said, "As long as we're speaking of ballet, I thought your ad for the public television special you're funding was lovely. But you know, it was in the wrong publication."

"Is that so?" His tone neither agreed nor disagreed, but the look in his eyes told Susannah she was on dangerous ground.

She raised her chin a trifle and went straight on. "The readers of that magazine are attuned to cultural events, and they probably already know about your program. Your target audience is much broader, and the advertising should be spread across general interest magazines instead."

"How very interesting." He glanced at his watch.

Susannah braced herself. Any second now, he was going to declare the interview over. It was maddening to know that she'd never had a fair shot—and even more frustrating to have to take every bit of the blame.

The intercom buzzed. Though Amos Richards made no effort to pick up the telephone, he brightened visibly—much to Susannah's surprise. "The CEO is on his way in," he said, and sat up straighter.

Relief surged through her. If there was a reason for the wait, then she wasn't out of the running. And if the CEO wanted to talk to her...

Behind Susannah, the office door opened. "Sorry to be late, Amos," a breezy voice said.

She swallowed hard, and turned—and looked straight at the chief executive officer of Universal Dynamics.

And Marc went on, "I got held up, you see, by a box of chocolates."

CHAPTER EIGHT

SUSANNAH's heart turned into a lump of ice as she stared at him.

Marc hadn't changed an iota—physically, at least—in the hour since she'd seen him talking his way past Mrs. Holcomb's door. He was still wearing the same pin-striped shirt and khaki trousers that he'd had on this morning at the museum. His sleeves were casually rolled to precisely the same point, halfway between wrist and elbow. He wore no jacket, no tie, and no wristwatch, and his shoes weren't executive wingtips but scuffed and comfortable-looking loafers. His hair was still engagingly ruffled by the breeze which had caressed him as he'd stood outside Tryad, chocolate box in hand.

And yet, something was different. Very different. Perhaps it was the way he stood, or the air of authority he wore. But there wasn't an ounce of doubt in Susannah's mind that he was exactly what Amos Richards had announced him to be.

Chief executive officer...

She had never really forgotten the cut of the suit he'd been wearing at Cyrus's funeral, or the initials mono-grammed on his cuff which had given her such a jolt at the party afterward. But it had been easy to push those memories aside. They'd been the exception rather than the rule, and each time she'd seen him in worn jeans and sneakers and T-shirts, the image of the elegant and tailored Marc had faded further into the distance.

Exactly as he'd intended. He must have had fun planning this, Susannah thought bitterly. Making it sound as if his job wasn't important enough to him to bother to

131

go back to. Talking about stumbling across the "Masterworks" show on public television—hadn't Universal Dynamics been a major sponsor for the last year or two? Or maybe even longer; she'd had no reason to notice until now.

Amos Richards stood up. "I'd like to introduce—"

Susannah had already started to speak. "What a snob you are, Marc Herrington!"

He actually looked startled. "Me? That's quite an accusation, coming from you. I've never said I'm better than anyone else."

"Oh, haven't you? Why do you want everyone to think you're some kind of a ignorant bumpkin, unless it's because that way you can feel superior? You may have turned snobbishness upside down, but you're still pretending to be something you aren't. That whole thing about Evans Jackson—"

"Just a minute. I wasn't pretending about thinking he's a fraud."

Susannah's thoughts had raced on. "And you wanted me to trust you!"

"It would be nice. After all, I'm considering trusting *you* with my public relations—"

"Sure you are," Susannah jeered. "And nuclear reactors are perfectly safe, too."

"Well, I suppose it depends on what we're comparing them to. Next to you, they look pretty tame, but I wouldn't exactly say—"

He could stand there and joke about it? That was the final straw. Almost automatically Susannah gathered up her handbag and the leather portfolio which represented so much wasted effort and started for the door.

She caught a last glimpse of Amos Richards as she left the office, and had to force down the hysterical desire to laugh at the unattractive way his mouth was hanging open.

She was almost to her car, her keys already in her hand, when Marc caught up with her. "Susannah! Can we at least talk about this?"

She wheeled to face him. "Talk about what? The way you set me up?"

"I haven't done anything of the sort. We really are looking at hiring a public relations firm. The whole operation is getting too big to handle in-house."

"And what do I have to go to get the job? Sleep with you?" Her voice was heavy with sarcasm. "No wonder Kit or Alison wouldn't do, only me. No doubt you expect me to be flattered because you're so determined to get your own way?"

"It's a legitimate job and a legitimate selection process." Somehow he'd moved between Susannah and her car. "Though I must admit it's going to be a trick persuading Amos, since he thought even before this little fiasco that you were too flighty even to consider."

"Oh, I'm sure you could convince him. I doubt Amos would fight you too hard. Who's in charge here, anyway?" She reached around him to unlock the driver's door, and added almost to herself, "And to think that I almost told you—"

"Told me what?" Marc's voice was soft, almost silky.

"Oh, no. I'm not as gullible as that." She tried to step around him to open the door.

Marc moved a few inches and blocked her way again. "What happened to the baby, Susannah?"

She looked skyward, as if for patience—or answers. "I doubt you'd believe me if I told you I was never pregnant, so—"

"Telling me you were having a baby, if you weren't, would have been a pretty stupid scam. Considering that we'd never made love and any baby of yours couldn't possibly be mine—"

"Quite right," Susannah said tightly. "How could I have overlooked something so obvious?"

Marc shook his head sympathetically. "Terribly bad planning on your part, Susannah, all the way through. If you had made love with me even once, so your child could have been mine as well..." His voice was low, and the rich tones seemed to stroke her skin like gentle fingers, teasing and exciting each cell along the way. "I'd have fallen oh-so-neatly into your trap."

"It might not have been good planning," Susannah snapped, "but it was lucky for me in the long run not to be stuck with you. Now if you don't mind, Marc, either move out of my way, or I'll go back inside and tell your receptionist to call the police because you're holding me hostage. And won't that look nice on the official record?"

Susannah went home instead of back to Tryad. She suspected that both Kit and Alison would still be at the office, anxious to hear about her appointment with Amos Richards, and she needed a little time first. Time to sort out what had happened. Time to figure out what to tell her partners.

Time to come to terms, herself, with the idea that Marc Herrington, one-time welder, was now the head of one of the world's most successful, profitable, and generous corporations...

The irony was stunning.

There'd never been any doubt about Marc's intelligence or his ability—but it was a long way from the factory floor to the top executive office, and it took more than intelligence and ability to make the climb. A certain amount of conformity was necessary for a young man working his way up through the ranks of a major corporation. Susannah would have said, without thinking twice about it, that Marc was far too independent, too much a free thinker, to conform long enough to survive the weeding-out process.

The man was just full of surprises, she told herself. Most of them less-than-pleasant ones.

In a feeble effort to keep herself from thinking, she plunged into cleaning her apartment. In the last couple of weeks, she hadn't spent much time at home. Dust had gathered, and mail was stacked high. She was washing the last of the coffee mugs which had collected in the kitchen sink when the doorbell rang, and she was already in the foyer on her way to answer the summons when she realized the time. Seven o'clock, on the dot—which probably meant that her visitor was Marc, come to remind her of their supposed dinner date.

She stopped in midstep. The bell pealed again, and then she heard his voice, muffled by the barrier of the door between them. "Susannah, I know you're in there. Your car's out in the parking lot. So I'm just going to sit out here and make noise until you answer or the neighbors complain to the building manager—whichever comes first."

She was tempted to call the manager herself and report a madman wandering the halls and harassing the tenants. Instead, she pulled the door open a couple of inches and said icily, "If I'd realized you'd actually have the gall to come here, I'd have picked up the doormat so you wouldn't get the idea that what it says applies to you."

Marc's eyes lit with a warm, sultry glow, and he inserted a well-worn loafer between door and jamb.

"And you couldn't have known for certain that I was here, either," Susannah went on. "I could have taken a cab, or gone out for a walk."

Marc shrugged. "In that case, I'd have felt a bit foolish, standing here talking to myself. But of course it wouldn't have been the first time. I thought you might prefer not going out for dinner—"

"You've got that much right."

"So I brought pizza."

The box he was balancing on his upraised hand like a waiter's tray emitted a marvelous aroma. Susannah hadn't realized how hungry she was; only now did she remember the box of crab rangoon which she'd abandoned untouched in her car. She'd have to remember to throw it out tomorrow, before its scent became a permanent part of the vehicle.

But hungry or not, there were limits. She'd rather eat cold, stale, dry toast. "No, thanks. Now if you'd take your foot out of the door…"

His smile faded, and the glow in his eyes dimmed a bit. But the foot remained. "Why does it bother you so much, Susannah?"

"It doesn't. Not at all."

"Oh, yes it does, or you'd have had to ask what I meant."

Susannah shrugged. "What else could you be talking about but your success? I'll admit I'd like to know how that came about."

"I'll tell you—over pizza."

"Personal connections?" Susannah mused. "Black-mailing someone high up in the ranks? Or perhaps your mother had *another* besotted old flame like Cyrus."

"Don't you think that would be a bit steep?"

"Since I never met your mother, how should I know? Or maybe it was Cyrus himself who pulled strings for you. The trouble is, you just don't seem the sort to climb the corporate ladder in the ordinary way. In fact, I'd have said you were more likely to be out swinging on a trapeze."

Marc shrugged. "That's just about how it happened."

He leaned against the door frame and looked down at her.

Obviously, he wasn't going to volunteer another word about how he'd come to work for Universal Dynamics, no matter how long he stood there. And just as obviously, he wasn't going away.

"You said yourself that you were researching your new client," Marc reminded, "and my connection with Universal Dynamics has never been any secret, so I thought you already knew—maybe even assumed that I wouldn't be involved in the process and planned to give me a jolt sooner or later. But I should have made sure before you got into Amos's office."

"Why? Because the scene I made this afternoon would make it harder for you to convince him to hire me? *If* I was interested in the account, which I assure you I'm not."

"I didn't instruct Amos to call Tryad, Susannah. I told you we've been considering an outside PR firm for months now."

"But you did give him my name."

"I mentioned it."

"And then you sat back to watch the fun."

"Something like that, yes," Marc admitted. His gaze was dark and steady, like a magnet holding her in place. She couldn't look away from him, but as she stared up into his eyes, her breathing and her heartbeat seemed to slow. Or was it instead that each moment seemed to stretch into forever?

Now I know why Mrs. Holcomb let him in, Susannah thought. *He hypnotized her.*

"If you're sorry," she heard herself say, "you should have brought chocolates."

The sparkle in his eyes came first, she saw, even before he started to smile. "Oh, no," he said. "No dessert till you've eaten every bite of your dinner."

Susannah didn't make a conscious decision to step back from the door; she didn't even realize she'd done it until he was inside, and then she could only watch as his gaze flicked over the small living room with its minimal furniture, framed Degas posters, and the single window with its view of another apartment building beyond.

She braced herself for his comment about the simple surroundings, but all he said was, "Which way to the plates?"

Susannah pointed to the kitchen. "You *have* acquired culture in the last eight years, haven't you? The idea of needing a plate in order to eat pizza...."

The dancing lights in his eyes belied his sober tone. "I don't bother when I'm on my own turf. But since it's not my upholstery and carpet, I thought perhaps I'd better be polite." He set the pizza box on the counter next to the pile of clean coffee mugs, broke off a still-steaming piece of pizza and slid it onto the plate Susannah handed him. But when he held it out to her, she shook her head.

"Don't tell me you aren't hungry," he argued. "You can't have had time for lunch any more than I did—and even though I benefitted from Mrs. Holcomb's cinnamon rolls, I'm starving."

"She makes cinnamon rolls?" It was no more than an idle question.

"From scratch, no less. But good and filling as they were, they didn't quite fill the gap." Marc reached for another plate. "There's no point in being a martyr, Susannah. Eat your pizza while it's hot."

Susannah sat down at the tiny kitchen table and toyed with the strands of cheese which dangled over the edge of her plate. "You were going to explain to me how on earth you ended up in charge of a major corporation," she reminded. "*Did* you blackmail somebody?"

"You sound doubtful that I could have achieved the position on my own merits."

"That's an understatement. I could see you as a team foreman, Marc, or maybe even a floor supervisor. But I can't imagine anyone in his right mind turning you loose in a head office—and the person who made you CEO must have been certifiably crazy."

"You're not the first one to wonder about that." Marc bit into a second piece of pizza. "Sometimes even I think I should have my head examined."

Susannah frowned. "Wait a minute. *You* made yourself…"

"It was not my choice to be the boss," Marc assured her. "Paperwork and budgets are not my favorite activity. My notion of a fun job is to sit somewhere with my feet on a drafting table and think—and then stroll out to a shop somewhere and see if I can make my idea work in the real world. That's how this whole thing started."

"Universal Dynamics? You mean—"

"I was laid off, just a few months after that infamous Thanksgiving when you took me home to meet the family. As a matter of fact, it was probably just about the same time the baby was due—and wouldn't your parents have been thrilled about that, if you'd had your way?"

Susannah picked the slices of black olive off her pizza and stacked them on the edge of her plate.

"It wasn't a permanent job loss, just one of the periodic downturns in the agricultural machinery business. The executives had—as they often did—overestimated demand. But the result was I had plenty of time on my hands for a few months, till I was called back to work. Plenty of time to wonder about all the pieces that were left over from the manufacturing process—scraps of metal, punched-out chunks of plastic, bits of wire—and consider what could be done with all those things."

"Recycling," Susannah said, and shrugged. "What's so new about that?"

"In a sense, you're right, but most recycling means reprocessing the materials—melting or shredding, or something else that takes energy and costs money. I wondered if there wasn't a use for those pieces just as they came off the line. And sure enough, one of the leftover pieces of a specialized composite was exactly the right size and thickness and chemical composition to be an insulator in household electrical appliances. And we threw them away by the thousands."

"An insulator?" Susannah repeated.

"In things like toasters and irons and hair dryers and griddles and a hundred other things. All it needed was to be bent at an unusual angle—which isn't quite as easy as it sounds. I offered to buy the waste from the company I worked for, rigged up a machine to make the bend just right, and sold each piece for at least a hundred times what I'd paid for it to a whole lot of other companies."

"All you did was bend—" Susannah shook her head.

"That's how it started. Now, of course, we're not just bending chunks of composite, we're selling the machines to do it—and a whole lot of other things, too."

"You didn't go to work for Universal Dynamics, you founded it?"

"That's about the size of it," Marc agreed.

"You didn't climb to the executive office, you started out there."

"Right. In those days I was also the production crew, the shipping department, the bookkeeper *and* the janitor. If I'd had any idea where it was going to lead—and which job I'd end up with—I might have just stuck to welding, so I'd have more time to play in my workshop."

Susannah didn't believe it for a minute. Marc might

say he hated all the administrative stuff, but he couldn't be so successful at something he detested. And he *was* obviously successful at managing his company—or Universal Dynamics wouldn't be making the zillions of dollars it gave away each year.

Marc added plaintively, "I've looked for an experienced CEO to actually run the place—but nobody seems to want to work for me. Middle management people are easy to find, but the really experienced executive types all say I'm a loose cannon."

"I can understand that," Susannah said dryly. "If you turned the place over to an expert, you'd probably be roaming the production floor contradicting all the head office's orders."

"Oh, I do that anyway." He polished off another piece of pizza and surveyed her plate. "Don't you like black olives anymore?"

Susannah picked up the pizza slice and made a pretense of taking a bite. "What I don't understand is why you pretended to be a poor relation. I mean, don't you think it was a bit much to actually move into Cyrus's house?"

"Why shouldn't I?" Marc said coolly. "I own the place now, and I needed to go through all of his papers, so it was just as practical to stay there. And since I didn't have a house before, it seemed a good opportunity to see what it feels like. A way to experience all the pros and cons of home ownership before I decide whether to keep it."

Out of the blue, she remembered a much younger Marc, shyly sharing his dream with her over a banana split at the campus ice cream shop, not long before that ill-fated Thanksgiving. All those years ago, the height of his ambition had been to own a ranch house somewhere in the suburbs, complete with a mortgage, a dog, a bit of lawn, and a long sidewalk where children could learn to ride bicycles...

It was utterly foolish, Susannah told herself firmly, to feel sorry that he had never achieved that particular dream. Sympathy for a man who must be a billionaire was obviously a waste of time; he could have acquired his fondest wish anytime in the last few years.

"Well, you've got the dog and the lawn now," she said crisply. "I'm sure you won't miss the mortgage, and you don't need the sidewalk, since there are enough miles of hallway inside Universal Dynamics to let a hundred little kids ride their bikes."

Marc paused, a slice of pizza suspended in midair, and looked thoughtful. "Now why didn't that idea ever occur to me? That would really make people like Amos sit up and take notice."

It isn't just you, Susannah, she told herself. *The man honestly enjoys tormenting people.* "You do realize it's no accident that anyone with choices doesn't want to work for you?"

But Marc obviously wasn't listening. "If we laid out a sort of figure-eight track around the offices, we could sponsor races to promote better fitness for America's youth... Wait till I tell Amos about your first suggestion to increase the public's awareness of the company."

"I don't think I want credit for it," Susannah said dryly. "But as long as you're working out details, don't forget the other advantages. Your employees couldn't go wandering off on coffee breaks or other nonproductive time-wasters, because if they so much as set foot outside their office doors they'd be run over."

"And then," Marc said sadly, "I'd probably have them complaining about tire marks on their clothes. Too bad—it sounded like such a good idea at first. But I'm sure you're only getting warmed up." He leaned back in his chair. "I'll tell Amos to expect great things from you. Which reminds me, you'll want to stay in touch with him.''

"Why?"

"Because I won't be terribly easy to find for a few days. I'd like to start on Cyrus's warehouse tomorrow, before I leave for Hawaii.''

"Hawaii?"

"You're a very harmonic echo, Susannah. Sort of like this trip, as a matter of fact. I thought all the details were in place two weeks ago when I came home for Cyrus's funeral, but now it seems I've got it all to do over.''

But hadn't Cyrus's attorney told Pierce that Marc was on vacation and wouldn't cut it short for the funeral? Or perhaps, Susannah thought, that had been only Pierce's interpretation of whatever Joe Brewster had actually said. Pierce had been in no mood to put a good spin on anything Cyrus's heir had done.

Anyway, why should she feel an odd vacancy in the pit of her stomach at the idea of Marc going away?

Because he'll be coming back, she told herself wryly. She picked up their plates and dumped the leftovers in the garbage.

Marc was looking meditatively around the apartment. "I don't suppose you're allowed to keep a dog here, are you?"

"Why would I want to?"

"I was just thinking about O'Leary. He's going to be awfully lonely without me.''

"So call some of Cyrus's staff back from their vacation.''

"That would be difficult.''

"Offended them that badly, did you?''

"Well, their sense of what was appropriate did have more in common with your mother's than with mine,'' Marc admitted. "Which reminds me, you never have told me anything more about your parents. I stopped by to see you over the weekend and one of your neighbors said you were spending the day with your mother."

"My neighbors," Susannah muttered, "are obviously too well informed."

"She thought you were probably on a shopping spree."

Susannah shot a sideways look at him. She couldn't detect even a hint of irony in his voice. "Actually," she said, "we were planning a dinner party."

"Of course. Why didn't I think of that? The Northbrook Millers have a position to uphold."

If he only knew, Susannah thought, how humorous it was—in a midnight-black sort of way—to talk of Elspeth Miller's need to maintain her position in society...

But of course that was the problem. If he were to find out, and he thought it laughable, Susannah knew she couldn't bear it.

Susannah was so early the next morning that she was stunned when her key clicked futilely in the lock and the front door swung open almost without effort. But the moment she was inside, she saw that Kit was perched on the corner of Rita's desk with a coffee mug in her hand, while Alison flipped through the contents of her mail basket.

"It's barely light outside," Susannah said. "What's with you two?" Not that she had to ask, exactly; if either Kit or Alison had been gone till late yesterday, trying to land a crucial new account, Susannah wouldn't have been hovering in Rita's office, waiting for news—she'd have been sitting on the front steps.

"We are comparing tummy troubles," Kit said grandly.

Susannah sent a blighting look toward Kit's mug.

"Surely you have more sense than to be drinking coffee on an upset stomach."

"Exactly what I told her," Alison muttered.

"Oh, coffee has never given me any trouble," Kit announced. "Personally, I think it's the Chinese food."

Susannah frowned. "You didn't try to eat it all, did you?"

"Heavens, no. What do you think we are, gluttons?"

"Well, count me out on the Chinese food theory." Alison finished sorting her mail and stacked it into neat piles. "I didn't even have a bite."

She did look a bit under the weather, Susannah thought. Alison's skin was usually as fair as porcelain, but today she was pure white.

"But that's the whole point," Kit said. "Just seeing it all was enough to make me ache."

Susannah bit the bullet; delaying the bad news wasn't going to soften the blow. "Well, I've got my share this morning, too. Of tummy troubles, that is."

Kit looked sympathetic. "It didn't go well, then?"

"Oh, Amos was just fine. We had a nice chat about the weather. Then I found out who owns Universal Dynamics, and—"

"Marcus Herrington," Alison said.

Susannah turned on her, wide-eyed. "You knew that, and you didn't warn me?"

Alison shook her head. "I didn't know it till about two this morning, when I was lying awake thinking about your appointment. I knew it hadn't gone well, because if it had been a success you'd have come back dancing a jig, so—"

"Susannah doesn't do jigs," Kit pointed out. "She's ballet trained, she pirouettes."

"Whatever. I reached for my *Dun and Bradstreet* and looked it up. And there, in black and white..."

"You keep *Dun and Bradstreet* beside your bed?"

Despite her own frustration, Susannah had to bite back a whoop of laughter at Kit's awed whisper.

"It's productive and relaxing reading," Alison said.

"No doubt it's better than sleeping pills," Kit murmured. "*And* a whole lot less habit-forming. Just be careful not to doze off and drop it on your nose, Ali, or you'll fracture your skull."

Alison made a face at Kit and came across the room to put an arm around Susannah. "Don't fret, Sue. Whatever happened, it obviously wasn't your fault—the deck was stacked against you. And we've done just fine without Universal Dynamics for three years. We can keep right on."

Susannah felt the prickle of hot tears, and tried to fight them back. "I don't deserve you two."

Kit slid off Rita's desk. "No, you don't," she said, and grinned. "But you're stuck with us, so you might as well get used to it!"

Susannah retrieved her briefcase and laptop computer, waved at Rita, who'd just arrived, and left the brownstone. Before she was off the porch, however, she was startled by a hoarse whisper from next door. "Miss!"

Over the dividing wall, she could see little more than Mrs. Holcomb's broom-straw-coarse hair and a pair of bright, beady eyes. "Are you going to see that young man of yours?" the old woman rasped.

"He's not mine, exactly," Susannah said cautiously. "But I'll see him, yes."

"Give him this." A hand reached around the corner of the porch to thrust an object at her. Susannah took it automatically, and the hand withdrew like a recoiling spring—as if Mrs. Holcomb feared that the early morning sunlight might make her skin shrivel up and vanish in a puff of dust.

Susannah found herself staring down at a plastic-wrapped plate heaped with cookies—evenly browned, identical in size, and so fresh from the oven that the china dish was hot against her fingers.

"Just what he needs," she muttered. "Another stroke for his ego!"

By the time she reached Cyrus's house, her car smelled of warm nuts and butter and sugar, and it was all she could do to keep her hands off Marc's treasure.

Marc had obviously been watching for her, because he pulled open the front door even before Susannah reached the porch. He eyed the plate in her hand and said, "Cookies? Home-baked cookies? I have to give you credit, Susannah. That's got an ordinary store-bought box of chocolates beat a mile. So what are you sorry for—or would you like me to guess?"

Susannah considered ramming the cookies down his throat, plate and all. "That I'm here, for one. But the cookies weren't my idea, they're courtesy of Mrs. Holcomb. Brother, did you snow her." She handed him the plate and submitted to O'Leary's ecstatic welcome. "Is he always this enthusiastic about visitors?"

"Just you and me—and where I'm concerned it doesn't matter if I've been gone all day or fifteen minutes. I told you, he'll break his heart if he has to go to a kennel while I'm gone." He fished a cookie out of the package and munched it. O'Leary sniffed and sat worshipfully at his master's feet. "You know, Susannah, I've been thinking."

"Dangerous habit. I'd recommend you cut it out immediately."

"You're really not going to sleep with me to get Cyrus's paintings for the Dearborn, are you?"

She looked up at him in wide-eyed awe. "Give the man a cigar! Has it actually taken you this long to understand that?"

"So let's raise the stakes."

"With what? Not the PR job, surely. I've already turned it down once."

"Only if bribery would work. No, on second thought, I'd much rather not toy with my business. I was thinking…" He snagged another cookie from under the plastic wrap and took a bite. "I was thinking that perhaps I ought to ask you to marry me."

CHAPTER NINE

THE porch floor revolved under Susannah's feet, wobbling like an antique merry-go-round. It was all she could do to force a single word through her dry throat, and the question rasped like a carpenter's file. "Why?"

Marc's eyebrows lifted. "You sound horrified."

No doubt she did. But even in the midst of her shock, Susannah realized that Marc appeared to be far more interested in her reaction than he'd been in the original question—though of course, it hadn't really been a question at all. He hadn't actually asked her to marry him. He hadn't even said, in so many words, that he'd decided to do so. He'd said, *Perhaps I ought to ask you...*

He hadn't sounded convinced, that was certain. And he hadn't looked like a man who was about to put himself on the line and perhaps change the course of his life, either. He certainly hadn't looked at her just now as he had eight years ago when he'd said something very similar...

The vision of him as he'd been in those days rose up before her. The young Marc had been vulnerable, eager, a bit shy—all characteristics that the man he had become seemed to have left behind.

The two faces—the young Marc and the mature one—overlapped before her, shifting and wavering. It felt as if she were looking through someone else's glasses and trying to bring a picture into focus. It was an impossible task, and the longer she tried to accomplish it, the more confusing the picture would grow. And the longer Marc would have to inspect her, to assess the results of his comment.

Smile, Susannah, she ordered herself.

Her lips felt tight and her smile fake, but she managed to keep her voice steady. "That's because I *am* horrified. It was bad enough when you only wanted to sleep with me, but this… What brought such a crazy idea to your mind?"

Marc set the plate of cookies on the porch rail, leaned against the door, and folded his arms across his chest. "It seems to be the next logical step, now that the business is well situated, to establish myself socially. I don't know why it took me so long to think of it, actually. As soon as I saw how respectfully all the dowagers treated you at the museum opening, it should have been obvious. The Northbrook Millers, you know."

"That's not—" Just a fraction too late, Susannah thought better of the comment and bit her tongue. Much as she longed to tell him that it was her own skills and not her family heritage which had won her respect from the Dearborn's staff and directors, she'd only be giving him information that could be used against her in the long run.

Marc paused, head tipped inquisitively.

"Nothing," Susannah said lamely.

"And of course, as you so helpfully pointed out last night, I'm just not very good at the slow and methodical route to success. So playing leapfrog by forming an alliance with the already-entrenched Millers seems a natural move."

He wasn't conscious of the irony in his words, Susannah knew, but nevertheless it left a bitter taste in her mouth and a crushing ache in her heart. "From your point of view, no doubt it would." Her voice was caustic enough to etch glass. "But then, of course, there's my outlook to consider. What's in it for me?"

"Now that's an excellent question," Marc mused. "Worthy of your mother, at her very best. Of course there's the money...but perhaps a little more is hardly an incentive if one already has plenty?''

"Is that your philosophy? I can see it might be where Universal Dynamics is concerned, of course, but then there's the way you reacted to Cyrus's legacy—dropping everything in order to make sure not a single penny was overlooked.''

"If I'm so grasping," Marc said mildly, "how do you explain me giving expensive paintings to museums and getting nothing in return?''

"One painting. A painting you hated. And I wouldn't say you got nothing in return. The amusement value alone—''

"That's true. I wonder if it would be as amusing to send Pierce another one." He considered, and shook his head. "No, I think we've wrung all the possible enjoyment out of that idea. It's time for something new.''

Susannah couldn't keep herself from drawing a long anticipatory breath and waiting in agony for whatever he might come up with next.

Marc didn't seem to notice, however. He'd returned, like a boomerang, to the original subject. "If money isn't enough to tempt you—''

"Believe me, it isn't.''

"Then perhaps you'd simply find it enjoyable?''

"Hardly. If that was the way my mind operated, I wouldn't have—'' She stopped abruptly, but it was too late.

Marc's eyes brightened. "You wouldn't have refused to sleep with me? Now that's an interesting development... Well, I'll just have to give it some thought. I'm sure somewhere there's a reason you'd find advantageous. Are we taking your car or mine down to the warehouse?''

The sudden tangent took Susannah off guard. "Mine, I guess. It's already out in the street.''

Marc whistled for O'Leary, who had finally given up begging for cookies and gone to sniff his way around the perimeter of the fence. The dog took the front steps at a leap, ignored the door Marc was holding open, and thrust his nose instead into the plate, forgotten on the porch rail.

Marc let go of the door and dived for the plate, but he was too far away to hope for success. Susannah, too, made a grab. She missed the plate by the width of a fingernail, and the china shattered against the wooden floor. The cookies spread out in a classic shotgun pattern amongst the china shards, and O'Leary's claws scuffed against the boards as he scrambled from cookie to cookie, gulping wildly.

"So much for his celebrated good behavior," Susannah pointed out. "Now we're all in trouble, breaking Mrs. Holcomb's plate just when she was starting to come out of her shell… You'll have to explain it to her, Marc, because I'm not taking the blame."

Only when the last cookie was gone did O'Leary look up at Marc, wave his plumed tail, and whine to be let inside.

"Don't even try to look innocent, you ungrateful mutt," Marc told him. "You've still got crumbs all over your chin. And to think I was going to try again to persuade Susannah to keep you so you wouldn't have to go to the kennel."

O'Leary's tail thumped hopefully against the porch rail as he turned 'round to Susannah, his brown eyes wide and worshipful.

She tried to ignore the appeal. The dog hadn't really understood, she told herself. He'd only been reacting to her name. "Maybe you should ask the vet to pump his stomach while he's in the kennel."

"Hear that, pal?" Marc asked the dog. "Now you've really shot your chances of staying out of puppy prison.

That's not a bad idea, though—having your stomach pumped might remind you to stay away from food that's intended for people.''

"I didn't mean it as a punishment," Susannah protested. "It's just that at the speed he ate those cookies, he might have inhaled part of the plate."

"Oh, no—not O'Leary. He's only dumb when being smart's a disadvantage, and he knows a whole lot better than to eat china under any circumstances. Come on, O'Leary. Drooling all over Susannah's shoes isn't going to improve your chances." He half-dragged the dog into the house.

Susannah picked up the broken china. Surprisingly, the plate hadn't smashed into bits; the shards were large, and they fit together neatly and firmly. Marc had been right; so far as Susannah could tell, not a single splinter was missing.

With the cookies gone she could see, painted on the china, a slightly shaky ring of daffodils. Susannah thought the design was not only amateurish but a bit garish, but it was obviously hand-painted. There was no doubt Mrs. Holcomb had sent her best—and it was equally sure that she was going to be very annoyed when her precious plate didn't come back.

She heard the muted chime of the security system as it came to life, and a moment later Marc reappeared, carrying a paper bag. He locked the front door, then carefully took each broken bit of china from Susannah's hands and put it in the bag.

He didn't say a word, and finally Susannah couldn't stand it anymore. "What are you going to do with the plate? Keep it as a souvenir? Throw it away and blame it on me? Or glue the pieces back together and hope Mrs. Holcomb doesn't look at it too closely?"

"None of the above." He folded the top of the bag, tucked it under his arm, and started down the sidewalk toward her car. "I won't have time to look for a replacement today, but by the time I get home, I'll have mercifully forgotten what this one looks like."

"I wouldn't want to try describing it to an antique store clerk myself," Susannah admitted.

"Antiques? I was thinking more in terms of the flea market. I'll drop it off there on the way to the warehouse, and by the time I get back from Hawaii—"

"It's hand-painted, Marc. They'll never find a match."

"Considering what the thing looks like, I'd say that's an advantage." Marc held the front gate for her. "But surely there's an adequate substitute somewhere."

Susannah had her doubts that Mrs. Holcomb would see it that way, but there was no point in arguing. "There's no reason you couldn't look around the flea market yourself. You don't have to spend the whole day in the warehouse, just get me started. And I'm sure you have plenty to do if you're leaving tomorrow."

"I'm flying out tonight, actually." He held her door and walked around the car to slide into the passenger seat. "And one of the big attractions of spending the day at the warehouse is that it has no telephone, so museum directors can't call."

"I did warn you," Susannah pointed out.

"And you were right. The competition for the collection has already started."

"Well, don't let me keep you from making your best deal."

"Don't worry," he said. "I won't."

Susannah chewed on her lower lip for a moment. He'd sounded almost offhanded. But had that casual comment really been a sort of threat?

Cyrus's warehouse turned out to be only a room he'd leased from a downtown art gallery. Susannah, relieved to hear that the sprawling, block-square accumulation she'd envisioned existed only in her imagination, was already mentally rearranging her schedule for the afternoon as the woman who ran the gallery showed them to the half-hidden storage room.

Marc produced a key, cautiously opened the door, and fumbled around the corner for a light switch.

Susannah stood on tiptoe to peer over his shoulder, and groaned. Cyrus's warehouse might be only a single room, but it was long, narrow, and jammed with canvases. Paintings were haphazardly stacked against every inch of wall, and there was barely enough room between the piles to wriggle through.

To add to the discomfort, the air was chilly and slightly dry; Susannah could hear the background hum of a climate-control system. Some paintings didn't hold up well in human conditions, and of course Cyrus would have made sure his collection received the best possible care.

Susannah sneezed, and told herself that it was probably not a good omen.

By the end of the day, Susannah was certain she'd never been so grimy. Some of Cyrus's paintings couldn't have been moved in a decade, for despite the climate control system's high-tech air filters, dust had accumulated on every exposed surface. The light wasn't the best, either, and in the farthest reaches of the room, she almost had to squint in order to write down the descriptions and dimensions that Marc relayed to her.

But finally he emerged from the dimmest corner, brushing his hands together. "I wouldn't guarantee it, but I think that's everything," he said.

"Hallelujah." Susannah sneezed for what felt like the millionth time.

Marc's fingertips brushed gently over her hair. "Poor

dear—and I didn't even let you have a break for lunch, just a take-out sandwich. How about a drink?''

''Irish coffee,'' Susannah said dreamily. ''Hot and strong, with a good kick.'' She emerged from the cramped room, set her clipboard aside, and flexed every muscle in her body, ending up in a ballerina-like stretch, balanced on her toes with her arms extended as far above her head as she could reach.

''Sounds good to... Oh, damn. If that's the correct time—''

Susannah followed his gaze to the stylized clock on the gallery wall. ''Are you sure it isn't a modern art piece, permanently stuck at six p.m. and called *Cocktail Hour?*''

''Have you considered a career as an artist, Susannah? You've got as much talent, and a whole lot more imagination, than Evans Jackson does.'' Marc reached for the pendant watch on the gold chain around her neck and held it up for her inspection. ''Unfortunately, it's really six o'clock, and I've barely got time to get to O'Hare to catch my flight.''

''No Irish coffee?'' She picked up her clipboard and followed him to the gallery's front door. ''I've been robbed. Do you need a ride to the airport?''

''I was going to call a cab. But if you'd take me—'' His smile was brilliant enough to light the entire Sears Tower. ''I just have to stop at the house long enough to pick up my suitcase, and—damn. I forgot about O'Leary.''

Susannah sighed. ''What kennel?''

''I hadn't actually called one. I didn't plan on spending all day up to my neck in paintings, and in any case I was still hoping you might... It's not just O'Leary who needs looking after, you see. It's the house.''

''That is why people install security systems.''

''And why they buy watchdogs,'' Marc agreed. ''But

if O'Leary has to be in the kennel instead of on guard duty—''

"It looks to me as if his specialty is keeping the house safe from things like plates of cookies, not burglars. Okay, okay. I'll keep an eye on things."

"You'll stay there, of course."

"Overnight, you mean? But—''

"That's great. O'Leary won't be lonely. And you can read Cyrus's catalog, too."

Susannah stopped dead in the middle of the sidewalk. "Wait a minute. You knew Cyrus had a catalog of his collection, and you didn't tell me?"

"I just found it yesterday, on the bottom shelf behind the desk in his study. It's ingenious, really—he'd had it bound to look like an unabridged dictionary. You don't mind if I drive, do you?"

Susannah absently handed over the keys and got into the passenger seat. "Why a dictionary?"

"For the sake of the boring cover, I suppose—so nobody would know the extent of his collection unless he wanted to show them."

"But if he already had the values—" She looked down at her hands. Dirt rimmed her nails and was ground into her skin.

Marc shook his head. "He had a list of what he paid—which is an entirely different question. Besides, we'd have had to do a complete inventory anyway, to make sure the catalog's accurate and up-to-date. And since it's not exactly the sort of thing you can tuck in your back pocket and carry around to do comparisons..." He parked the car in front of Cyrus's house, the engine running. "I'll be back in a minute."

The trip to O'Hare went surprisingly quickly, considering the flow of rush-hour traffic. Obviously, Susannah thought, Marc knew all the shortcuts. Outside the terminal, he pulled up under a sternly worded No Parking sign and got out of the car.

"And you complain about me parking by fire hydrants?" Susannah muttered.

By the time she'd walked around the back of the car, Marc had lifted his suitcase out of the trunk. He held the driver's door for her, but instead of immediately shutting it, he stood looking down at her for a moment.

Warily, Susannah shot a glance up at him. It was silly to feel trapped in her seat, but she had to admit she did. His eyes were dark and serious—or was that an illusion caused by the glaring lights overhead? He bent closer, and her heart began to thud heavily. She didn't want him to kiss her...or did she?

The mischievous light was back in his eyes. "Feel free to use my pajamas," he said gently, and before she could answer he'd closed the car door and was approaching the terminal. At the entrance he turned and smiled and waved, with an easy assurance that made Susannah grit her teeth because it so clearly said that he'd known she'd be watching. And then he was gone.

"Pajamas," she said crossly. "I'd be amazed if he owned any!"

Marc hadn't been joking about the size and weight of Cyrus's catalog; when Susannah found it, it was covering a good part of the coffee table in the back parlor, which he'd set up as a sort of den. She gave the enormous volume a glance but decided to put off any close inspection until she'd settled in. First, she'd put her frozen pizza in the oven. Then she'd go upstairs and choose a bedroom, get out of her grimy clothes and into something comfortable, and come back down to eat her dinner and—perhaps—to browse through Cyrus's record of his collection.

O'Leary, obviously thrilled to see her again, insisted

on guarding every step she took. She almost tripped over him between dining room and kitchen, and he dashed up and down the stairs a half dozen times before she'd reached the hallway at the top.

She knew, from the time she'd spent studying the art in every room, that Marc was using the big bedroom at the front of the house. She deliberately turned the other way instead, toward a smaller guest room, rather than even walk past his door.

Use my pajamas, he'd said. As if she would!

She was curled up on the couch in the back parlor, enjoying the luxury of a satin dressing gown against clean and pampered skin, munching pizza, and flipping through a magazine—Cyrus's catalog could wait a little longer—when the telephone rang. Warily, she reached for it.

"Did you find the pajamas all right?" Marc asked.

Automatically, Susannah clutched at the low neck of her dressing gown, and then told herself not to be ridiculous. "Where are you?"

"I don't know. Somewhere over the Rockies, I expect."

"They put telephones on airplanes for business, Marc."

"As long as my credit card's good, I doubt anybody will cut off the connection. Don't you want to know why I called?"

"I assumed it was to check whether I was really here. Do you want to talk to O'Leary and make sure I'm doing things right?" The dog rolled his eyes at the sound of his name, but he didn't take his chin off Susannah's knee.

"No, thanks. I'm sure he's quite content with you. Do you have everything you need?"

"I'm quite comfortable."

"It is a nice house, isn't it? I've been thinking about

our discussion earlier today. If sheer fun isn't enough and you're looking for something more substantial, maybe Cyrus's house—''

It was just a game, she reminded herself. And Marc had not only made the rules, he was playing from a very safe distance. ''It's certainly substantial,'' she agreed lightly. ''But there's far too much furniture to dust. Sorry, but that's not what I'm looking for at all.''

''Hmm. Then perhaps you'll fall in love with O'Leary. A couple of days of him worshiping you and you'll be head over heels.''

''And marry you to get joint custody? No, I'm afraid O'Leary isn't nearly substantial enough, either.'' Susannah shifted the telephone to her other hand and toyed with a leftover slice of pizza.

''He is a bit dim when it suits him, but there's something very attractive about blind loyalty. All right, it's not the house and not the dog, so what else could—''

Distraction, she told herself. *That's the ticket.* ''While I'm down at the warehouse tomorrow, would you like me to choose something to hang where you took the Evans Jackson down? It left sort of a big blank hole on the wall.''

Triumph resounded in Marc's voice. ''I've got it— you wanted the Evans Jackson, and *that's* why you're so certain there's nothing which would tempt you to marry me, now that it's gone.''

''Of all the ridiculous—''

He went straight on as if she hadn't said a word. ''Do you suppose I can get it back so I can give it to you as a wedding present? If I was to offer Pierce everything else in Cyrus's whole collection in exchange... I absolutely won't hang it where I have to look at it every day, though.''

''Marc, would you quit playing this stupid game?''

The silence which followed was just long enough for

Susannah to regret losing control of her tongue. Then Marc said gently, "Oh, no, I'm enjoying it far too much to stop now. Shall we explore the question of why it's bothering you?"

Susannah gritted her teeth. Then she said sweetly, "Darn. And I was *so* looking forward to using the Evans Jackson to line the canopy above our bed."

Marc was still laughing when she hung up on him.

She jumped up, and O'Leary groaned in protest at being dislodged. With the remainder of her pizza in hand, Susannah headed for the kitchen. She'd clean up the mess and then really settle in to work on Cyrus's catalog. If she stayed busy, she wouldn't be tempted to think about Marc's nonsense.

Shall we explore why it's bothering you?

She stopped so suddenly that a couple of pieces of pizza slid off the pan and smacked onto the kitchen floor. O'Leary, at her heels, sniffed at it and obligingly mopped up the mess.

She knew, of course, why Marc's offhand nonsense had bothered her so. She'd known it for days, maybe weeks. Perhaps even from the moment she'd looked up from the monogram on his cuff into his eyes.

If pressed, Susannah would have admitted even to him that through all these years Marc had continued to live in her heart. Her memories of the old Marc—the idealistic and charming young man who hadn't yet shed all his naïveté—had remained tucked away in a corner, a souvenir of a long-lost love. Those sentimental memories would have stayed in the farthest closet in her mind forever, if the new, brash, incredibly self-assured Marc hadn't yanked open the door, walked straight in, and trampled them.

But then, instead of walking away from the wreckage, he'd stayed there, solidly planted in her heart.

That, Susannah would have denied to her last breath.

She *had* denied it, quite efficiently and even to herself, for some time, but she could do so no longer.

She had cared for the old Marc, as a girl cared...but she loved the new one.

"I want it not to be a game," she whispered. "I want him to come home to me. To love me."

Saying the words aloud gave them a solidity that weighed on her like a concrete yoke around her neck, for that sort of understanding was as far away now as it had been eight years ago. Farther, perhaps, with the shadows of time fallen between them.

Eight years ago, with the self-centered confidence of youth, she had picked herself up and gone on, certain that she would heal, that this crushing blow would pass, that there was someone else—someone better—waiting for her somewhere in the world. She'd never found that person, of course, because she'd been wrong; there had been no one else, no one better. Just the memories of Marc.

Now there was a new Marc. The naïveté was gone, but the idealism was still there, though it was better hidden. And the charm...there was no denying the charm. He was harder-edged now, even a little dangerous...and incredibly more attractive.

And she knew that this time she couldn't pretend that she'd get over it. This time, loving him was forever.

Susannah was in the antique store across the street from Cyrus's warehouse on Friday afternoon, paying for a dusty hand-painted plate, when her cellular phone rang. Since it was buried in her handbag, it rang several times before Susannah managed to dig it out.

Alison said, "I was just about to panic."

Susannah frowned, concerned. "You never panic, Ali. You were levelheaded in your playpen."

"Sue, I'm sorry." Alison's voice broke. "The nursing

home called. Your mother's developed pneumonia. She's much, much worse—and they want you to come.''

In a split second, Susannah's brain kicked into high gear, competently listing the things she'd have to do, efficiently ranking them in order of importance—and coolly denying any emotion which threatened to rear its head. She counted her change and put it away, picked up O'Leary at the house, repacked the few clothes she'd brought with her, and delivered the dog to Alison at the brownstone, all in an icy calm.

Alison looked more upset than Susannah herself felt. ''You shouldn't be driving,'' she said. ''If I didn't have a meeting this afternoon that I can't cancel—''

''I'm fine.'' Susannah looked over Alison's shoulder toward the back of the hallway and smiled faintly at the sight of Tryad's calico cat, hissing and spitting and backing a shuddering O'Leary into a corner. ''Some guard dog he is,'' she said. ''You're going to have your hands full here without worrying about me.''

Alison followed her out onto the porch. ''Maybe Kit can—''

Susannah shook her head and gave Alison a quick hug. ''Thanks for caring, Ali. But I'll be all right, really.''

She got through the two-hour drive to Rockford by not thinking at all, and even the first few hours at her mother's bedside would be forever blurry in Susannah's mind. Elspeth drifted in and out of consciousness, and even when she was awake it was hard to catch her words, harder still to tell if she knew where she was.

Susannah spent the night in the chair beside her mother's bed, refusing the staff's offer of an empty room down the hall. The nursing home was never completely quiet, but sounds were muted with the darkness, and Susannah sat upright, hands folded on the protective rail of Elspeth's bed, listening to each rasping breath and studying her mother's profile.

To society, Elspeth Miller had been elegant and aristocratic, always knowing what was proper, and never falling short of that standard. In her daughter's eyes she had been domineering, overbearing, and controlling, determined that Susannah would follow the path laid out for her.

It was no wonder, of course, that Susannah had reacted badly to that sort of tyranny. The only surprise was that her revolt hadn't been earlier and stronger, and that it hadn't carried even worse consequences....

In the long hours of the night, Susannah watched her mother's face. Elspeth had never been the cookie-baking sort of mother Susannah had envied her friends for having. She had been the last woman the young Susannah would have thought of as a confidante. And even as Susannah reached adulthood, they had never come close to the sort of grown-up friendship some mothers and daughters did.

But in her own way, within her own limitations, Elspeth had been the best mother she could be.

As the early light crept through the blinds to tint the walls the color of sunrise, peace crept into Susannah's heart. Her grip on the rail loosened, her head drooped, and she slept.

She didn't know how long she slept, but when she roused dawn had given way to full light and the hall was bustling with the normal morning traffic of medications and breakfast and baths. But it wasn't the noise which had awakened her; Susannah knew the instant she opened her eyes that it was her mother's gaze which had brought her back to awareness.

Elspeth was lying very quietly, looking at Susannah as if she hadn't ever seen her before. "I've been ill," she murmured.

There was no hint of the usual querulousness in her voice, only a hint of surprise. And in her dark eyes was a look of clarity that Susannah hadn't seen since before she'd brought her mother to Rockford.

"Yes," she said unsteadily. "You're better now."

Elspeth seemed to consider that. She looked around the room and gave a little nod as she turned back to her daughter. "You look tired, Susannah. Go and rest. The nurses will look after me."

Susannah was stunned by the matter-of-fact tone. Had this bout with serious illness actually served to clear Elspeth's mind? How much did she understand, and remember? Would the effect last?

She stood up, less interested in rest than in seeking out the nursing supervisor to share this new development. But Elspeth reached for her hand, and Susannah turned back to the bed.

"That young man..." Elspeth murmured.

Susannah's thoughts were already down the hall in the nursing station. "What man, Mother?"

"The one you insisted on marrying."

Susannah frowned. In the eight years since the fiasco, Elspeth Miller had only once referred to Marc—on Susannah's last visit. She must be picking up vibrations from Susannah's own thoughts, and garbling them.

"I'm so sorry," Elspeth whispered.

Susannah said carefully, "About Marc?"

"No. About the baby."

Susannah's heart plunged to her toes. *Oh, Mother,* she thought helplessly. *Please don't do this. Not now...*

"About us...your father and me...not wanting your baby. Susannah—won't you bring her to see me?"

The grip on her hand was surprisingly firm. Susannah looked down at her mother's face—thin, worn, with dark circles under the eyes. Not recent illness but years of pain had formed those lines. Perhaps, Susannah thought,

Elspeth hadn't been able to run as far away as they had all thought she'd done.

She patted her mother's hand. "If that would make you happy," she said, her voice low and soft, "then yes...when you get better, I'll bring her to see you."

Elspeth sighed, and relaxed, and closed her eyes.

From the hallway came a different sort of sound, and Susannah turned her head with a jerk. Marc stood in the doorway, a sheaf of fresh-cut flowers in one hand, his eyes as cold and dark as the back side of the moon.

Slowly, he extended the flowers to arm's length and dropped them in the nearest wastebasket. Then he stepped back into the hall and tugged at the edge of the door. With a tiny whisper, it began to close behind him—so slowly that he was long gone down the hall before the latch clicked shut.

CHAPTER TEN

SUSANNAH was through the door and down the hall before she had made a conscious choice to move at all. Still, she must have sat stunned for longer than she'd realized, for Marc was nowhere in sight.

A small voice inside her said, *It's just as well. You don't even know what you want to say to him.* But her body didn't seem to get the message; she skidded around the corner to the main lobby—and there he was, standing by the front door with a hand already on the knob.

She stopped, and as if alerted by the sudden cessation of running feet, Marc let his hand drop and turned toward her.

His jaw was set, his face rigid and so cold that Susannah could feel her heart freezing. Then anger surged through her, its heat washing away the chill. "Go ahead and leave," she said. "It's what you do best."

For an instant she thought he hadn't heard her, and when he spoke his voice was oddly gentle. "If that's what you came out here to tell me, Susannah, why did you bother?"

There was no answer to that—or at least no answer which wouldn't simply invite further questions—so she attacked again. "You didn't have to sneak around, Marc. You could at least have announced yourself."

"And interrupt an intimate conversation—and a long overdue one, from the sounds of it—between you and your mother?"

Her shoulders sagged. "What are you doing here, anyway?"

"When I got back early this morning there was a message from Alison that she'd taken O'Leary home with her. She sounded a little desperate, so I went straight over to pick him up. She told me why he was there, and about your mother—and I drove out here to hold your hand and offer comfort. Funny, isn't it?''

''Hilarious,'' Susannah said grimly.

''I meant odd—that after asking so many times, and actually beginning to believe you when you said there'd never been a child, I'd walk into that particular conversation. If you expect me to apologize for my poor timing, I'm afraid you're going to be disappointed again.'' His gaze was level, and his voice was absolutely flat. ''You lied, Susannah.''

And once again, she thought, *you've made assumptions, Marc.* And he was obviously no more interested in listening now than he'd been eight years ago.

There were some things about him which hadn't changed after all.

Something cracked inside her. She'd thought all those years ago that he'd broken her heart—but in fact he'd saved that treat for now. And he hadn't just shattered it, he was grinding the fragments into the dirt under his feet.

She looked at the door frame above his head and told the absolute and literal truth. ''You're right, Marc. I lied.''

She'd thought his jaw was tightly set before. Now a statue carved from granite would look cuddly in comparison. ''If you chased me down the hall just now to tell me about your daughter...''

Susannah shook her head. ''Oh, no. You've already assumed the worst—so why should I try to explain? No doubt your imagination can make the story far more exciting than the truth, anyway.''

''There are no explanations which could be adequate, and I didn't ask for any.''

She couldn't stand it anymore. "No, you didn't. It's the same thing all over again, Marc. You wouldn't listen to me then, and I won't give you the satisfaction of begging for your attention now." She turned on her heel and strode across the lobby, back toward her mother's room—and she didn't look over her shoulder.

Elspeth's face was peaceful and her breathing easier than it had been since Susannah arrived. She stood at the door for a full minute, watching her mother sleep. Then, as if compelled, she reached into the wastebasket and gathered up the cellophane-wrapped sheaf of flowers. They were carnations, mostly—red and white ones surrounded by asparagus fern—the kind of simple bouquet that supermarkets kept on hand for last-minute purchasers when florists' shops weren't open.

She sank down into her chair once more and laid the blooms across her knees. A couple of the carnations had broken in the fall, and their spicy scent rose from the crushed petals to torture her senses. But she couldn't bring herself to take them out of the room.

He had come to her, to be with her in a painful time—but what devil's prank had made him walk in at that particular moment? In that instant as he stood in the doorway and listened, time had folded together. It might have been eight years ago, on a crisply cold November day, after a walk in the cemetery. A day that had altered Susannah's world forever...

She hadn't even seen it coming. All she understood, as they strolled hand in hand along Northbrook's streets that afternoon, was that her knees were still weak from the way Marc had kissed her. There was a sparkle in Marc's eyes as well—half amusement, half awe—that could only have come from the same cause.

In the shadow of the Millers's front door, in the last private moment before they went inside, he'd drawn her close and kissed her again, and Susannah had melted against him just as her father opened the door and her mother, well-wrapped against the winter's wind in her favorite mink coat, had stepped over the threshold and stopped dead.

"How perfectly vulgar," Elspeth said, and the sarcasm which oozed from her voice made the words an insult worse than any amount of name-calling could have been. Her gaze flicked across Marc and dismissed him as she focused on her daughter. "Of course, I shouldn't expect anything else from you, Susannah, considering the sort of trash you've picked up—and dared to bring home."

It was the first time Elspeth's hostility had bubbled to the surface, but Susannah had known from the beginning of their visit that her mother was simmering. The moment Susannah introduced Marc, Elspeth had compared his aristocratic-sounding name to the hard callouses on his palm and asked suspiciously exactly what it was he did. And Marc—who had never before encountered anyone quite like Elspeth Miller—had told her proudly about his last promotion, to the most sophisticated welding machine on the assembly line. Elspeth's eyes flared, but she prided herself on being a lady. If it killed her, she would be polite to a guest in her house.

She hadn't even raised her voice—she was too cultivated for that—when she saw her daughter on the front steps wrapped in the arms of a man she would have called a common laborer. But once Marc had proved her opinion of him by behaving in so crude a way, she felt no further obligation to be polite. In her well-bred voice, she had told Susannah precisely what she thought of her behavior, and Marc exactly how rude it was to consider himself good enough to touch a Northbrook Miller. And, with that out of the way, she had proceeded to inform him about every other way in which he came up short of Miller standards, from family background to education to general intelligence to common sense to good taste...

Susannah's father hadn't added to the melee, but he hadn't interfered, either. When in annoyed boredom Susannah let her gaze drift his way—and caught him nodding approvingly as his wife finished telling Marc how blindingly unsuitable he was—she'd had enough.

But she wasn't the one who broke the silence after Elspeth finally ran out of words. It was Marc who said, very quietly, "Have you finished, Mrs. Miller?" When she answered only with a glower, he squared his shoulders and said, "Then there's something I'd like to tell you. You may find me not to your taste, but there's only one person whose opinion of me matters, and that's Susannah. I want to marry your daughter, and if—"

Susannah didn't honestly know whether she had loved him before that; she only knew that his kisses could send her blood pressure soaring and make her stop thinking of anything but him. But she loved him then, for the sheer courage it took to face Elspeth Miller in a coldly civilized rage and face her down. Susannah didn't know another man who could have done it.

For an instant, as Susannah looked with new eyes at Marc Herrington, she forgot about her father. She was soon reminded. If Charles Miller had swallowed a lighted cherry bomb, his explosion couldn't have been stronger. Even Elspeth's eyes widened at the sight, and before he was halfway through, she'd put a hand on his sleeve and said something feeble about the language he was using. He shook his wife off and went on castigating Marc for his nerve in daring to think of marrying a girl like his daughter, and that was when Susannah blew up.

"Of course I'm going to marry him," she said. "Why do you think I brought him home with me this weekend, anyway?"

Charles Miller didn't miss a beat. "And throw your

life away for a simpleton who'll never amount to anything?''

At the same instant, Elspeth said, "I absolutely forbid it.''

And the worst idea of Susannah's life popped full-fledged into her mind. It was not only the worst of the nineteen years she'd lived to that point, but the stupidest notion she could possibly create even if she spent a lifetime seeking out suggestions for bad plans.

"Well," she said calmly, "I'm afraid you can't do much about it, Mother. I have to marry Marc, you see—because I'm pregnant.''

The silence that descended was as complete as the utter quiet of outer space. Her father was the color of an eggplant; Susannah thought he was going to pop a major blood vessel. Elspeth reeled and then caught herself. Obviously, Susannah thought, she'd realized the disadvantages of fainting where the only surface to receive her was hard, cold ceramic tile.

"Well, that does put a different face on things," Charles Miller said grimly.

"You can say that again." Marc's voice sounded as if he'd had all the wind knocked out of him.

Susannah turned to give him a reassuring grin, to share the joke—and was stunned by the black coldness of his eyes...

Elspeth had thrown her shreds of remaining civility to the wind and started to scream like a first-class fishwife. Charles had shaken his finger under Susannah's nose and begun to lecture. She didn't even know how long it went on, except that it was a couple of hours later before she had a chance to get Marc alone.

She found him, finally, in the guest room he'd occupied for the weekend, tossing his belongings into his duffel bag with less care than she'd ever before seen him show for his possessions.

"Good idea," she said. "After the way they talked to you—*and* to me—leaving is the only thing to do. Let them cool off for a while and maybe they'll resemble humans again. I'll get my bags."

"Where are you going?" The question was careless, as if he wasn't interested in her answer.

"With you," Susannah said quietly. "Of course."

Marc didn't look up from his shaving kit. "I didn't invite you."

"But...but after that, I can't stay here."

"That is entirely your problem." He zipped his duffel bag and slung it over his shoulder. "You got yourself into this mess—maybe not alone, but it's damned sure I had nothing to do with it. And you can get yourself out."

"You said you wanted to marry me." Her voice sounded hollow, even to her own ears.

"That was before I knew what you're capable of."

"Marc, it's not what you think. If you'd just listen, try to understand—"

"I understand that you thought I'd be a handy patsy, so head over heels in love that I'd do anything for you. What's the matter with the real guy? Is he one of those high-society types who doesn't have the guts to take the heat for what he's done?"

Susannah had stared at him for a long moment. "Fine," she said, and tried to ignore the crack in her voice. "Go ahead and leave. Get lost. I'd never have gone through with it, anyway. You are absolutely hopeless, Marc Herrington—"

"Oh, I get it. You threw me into the soup so your parents will shed happy tears when you tell them I'm not the father after all. Good thinking, Susannah. They might even overlook your child's unorthodox beginnings, if the pedigree's all right in the end."

And he had gone out of her life, into the cold

November wind. Susannah only wished he had stayed out of her life...

She looked down at the carnations in her lap and realized that she was stroking the velvety softness of a fringed red petal. She jerked away as if the flower were fire instead.

He'd said, *I'd actually started to believe you...*

But in fact, nothing had changed. He had once more judged her without waiting for an explanation. That was a good part of what had divided them before, and despite the years it still lay between them. And in a sense, the gap was even wider now than it had been when she was one of the Northbrook Millers, and he was a welder in a farm-machinery factory.

Susannah spent the rest of the weekend in Rockford, but by Sunday evening, with Elspeth once more stable and back to organizing her own off-kilter world, she drove back to Chicago. Listless, depressed, and exhausted, she stayed in bed instead of going to the partners' Monday morning planning session, and stumbled into Tryad a couple of hours late.

Alison, who was coming down from the top floor production room with a poster design under one arm, made a detour into Rita's office, where Susannah was flipping through her accumulated mail, to inspect her. "You look like a sleepwalker."

"I feel like one, too. I'm sorry about skipping the meeting this morning, but—"

Alison shook her head. "Don't fret about it, because you didn't miss much. Kit spent most of the time in the ladies' room throwing up, and I suspected for a while that I..." She hesitated, as if she'd thought better of whatever she'd meant to say, and smoothly changed the subject. "Kit told me your mother's better."

Susannah nodded, and made a mental note to keep an

eye on Alison. As soon as she had some energy back, she'd have to find out what that half sentence had meant. Kit was a concern, too, of course—but Alison had sounded almost frightened, and that was very much unlike her. "Mother's back to her old imperious self. I talked to Kit yesterday afternoon, and she sounded fine then. What's the deal?"

"Well, I doubt her problem's contagious," Alison said dryly. "There should be a couple of messages in that mess from Amos Richards at Universal Dynamics. Maybe that deal isn't quite dead yet, after all?"

Susannah's heart rose to her throat, and then plummeted. It was Monday morning; those messages had probably come in last week—before her encounter with Marc at the nursing home—which made them ancient history. And even if Amos *had* called just this morning, she'd guarantee he wasn't passing along good news. "I'll check on it. But don't get your hopes up, Ali."

Upstairs in her office, she dropped the bundle of mail and messages on her desk and reached into her briefcase for her calendar. Instead of smooth leather, her fingertips touched a rustly paper bag, and she frowned.

She'd forgotten, in her concern for her mother, about the plate she'd bought for Mrs. Holcomb. It was handpainted with pink tulips, not daffodils, but they were just as off-center, just as wobbly. As a replacement for Mrs. Holcomb's splintered treasure, it wasn't half bad. As a gesture of thoughtfulness toward Marc, on the other hand...

She'd told herself even as she inspected the plate that she'd gone looking only to relieve him of a petty errand. But it wasn't true. She'd done it because she loved him... And, her conscience murmured, perhaps to show him how much he needed her. But at least Marc didn't know about the plate; he would never know exactly how foolish she had been.

But what was she to do with an amateurish hand-painted plate? Toss it into the wastebasket? She couldn't take it back, and she absolutely wouldn't keep it around as a reminder.

And in any case, the whole mess hadn't been Mrs. Holcomb's fault, so why should she be deprived of a replacement?

It was clear that she wasn't going to get much work done, so she might as well take care of this loose end instead. Susannah picked up the paper bag and went down the stairs and around by the sidewalk to knock on Mrs. Holcomb's door.

She knocked twice, and just as she was about to give up, the door creaked open a bare inch, just enough to let a suspicious eye peer through.

"Mrs. Holcomb," Susannah said. "About your plate... I'm very sorry, but there was an accident." She held out the crumpled bag. "I've brought you another plate, but I know how special that one must have been, and..."

"Not at all," Mrs. Holcomb said. Dark, beady eyes surveyed Susannah from head to toe. "You look like you're about to drop, girl. That young man of yours giving you trouble?"

"Not anymore," Susannah said dryly. "And he never was mine, really." She held out the bag. "This one has tulips instead of daffodils, I'm afraid."

"Tulips, eh? They're my very favorite flower." Mrs. Holcomb cradled the bag against her chest. "I think it's time for you to run along, now."

It was silly to feel rejected, just because Marc had been invited in to be fussed over and she had not. But Susannah felt a bit glum as she turned away from Mrs. Holcomb's door, head down. The woman could have said thanks, at least...

There was a shadow across the porch. Susannah's

head jerked up, and her heart jolted at the sight of Marc standing on the top step. Cradled in his arm was a plastic grocery bag, and inside it she could see the familiar shape of a plate. No wonder Mrs. Holcomb had been anxious for her to go, with a more interesting visitor in the offing.

"Excuse me," Susannah said. "I wouldn't want to interfere with your visit." *And with any luck,* she thought, *by the time Mrs. Holcomb's finished stuffing him with cinnamon rolls, I'll be halfway across Chicago.*

Not that it really mattered, of course, whether she headed for the state line or went back to her office. There was nothing left to say, and Marc knew it as well as she did. She could simply sit down on Mrs. Holcomb's front step and the most he'd do would be trip over her.

She headed instead for the safety which Tryad represented.

Marc cut her off at the front door. One moment he was on Mrs. Holcomb's front porch; in the next, he'd vaulted across the dividing wall and landed in front of Susannah.

"Cute," she said. "Obviously you didn't miss any workout sessions while you were in Hawaii. Excuse me."

He sidestepped and blocked her path. "I'm not going away, Susannah."

"I can't think of another thing we have to say to each other."

"How about the truth?" His voice was quiet, but it was not gentle.

"I've told you the truth."

"Which time?"

"Take your choice." She stepped to one side.

This time he let her slip past him, but as the doorknob turned under her hand he said, "I've always wondered, you know."

"What? Who the father was?" She couldn't quite keep her bitterness under control.

"No. I wondered whether your parents had disowned you. If you were all alone. Whether you'd been able to go back to college. If you and the baby were all right."

She looked over her shoulder at him, startled by what could only be sadness in his voice—and the icy lump which was her heart warmed by the fraction of a degree. If he had thought of her through the years...

If there was an invitation in that glance, Susannah was unaware of it—but Marc seemed to see one, for he followed her inside. She had to hold on to the railing as she climbed the stairs to her office, knowing he was only a step behind.

Maybe he really had cared for her, or perhaps he had simply felt guilty for reacting so quickly, without even hearing her side of the story. In any case, whatever he'd felt eight years ago was long gone now, and whatever he might have been starting to feel in the last few weeks had been blasted into oblivion in Elspeth's room two days ago. Susannah had put her foot in her mouth once more, and the result was the same as it had been before. It made no difference, really, that this time she had said what she did for the best of motives—to ease her mother's pain—instead of with the spite and anger which had prompted her original announcement. She had once more cost herself what she wanted most in the world...

No, she thought. She was not going to take all the blame. He had incredible nerve, refusing to listen to her on Saturday, and then showing up two days later demanding the truth...

"So what are you going to do about it? Take a child to see her?" he said. He stood just inside her office door, hands on his hips, gaze roving the room.

Susannah had been wondering that herself. "I don't

know. Just wait and see whether she regains her strength,
I suppose.''

"And whether she even remembers asking?'' He
wasn't looking at her but at the Degas poster on the far
wall.

"How did you know—'' Too late, she stopped herself. He might only have meant that no matter how ra-
tional they were under normal circumstances, people
who were very ill sometimes didn't remember what they
said. She tossed herself down on the couch and ran long,
nervous fingers through her hair.

"You could borrow one of the neighborhood girls, I
suppose.'' His voice was matter-of-fact. "There must be
several who are about the right age.''

"Yes, you've mentioned that fact before. I suppose
you think I can't produce my own child because I murdered her and buried her in a rose garden somewhere?''

"No. I think when you said you lied, you meant it
wasn't me you'd lied to, but your mother.'' Slowly, as
if he were approaching a wild animal, he settled on the
far end of the couch. "How long has she been delu-
sional?''

"Did Alison tell you that, too?'' She must have; only
Kit and Alison knew that one of the attractions of the
nursing home in Rockford was that no one there remembered the way Elspeth Miller had once lived. No one
there could remind her of everything she had lost. But
Susannah felt thoroughly confused; if Marc had known
that much before he came to Rockford, shouldn't he
have been more understanding?

Marc shook his head. "She didn't breathe a word.
What you said in the lobby that day—about how I hadn't
listened to you, and how the thing I did best was to walk
out—stung a bit.''

"Fancy that,'' Susannah said.

"So I didn't leave the nursing home right away, I

stayed around and talked to people. It didn't take much effort to pick up the rough edges of the story, but the details would have come a little harder—and it didn't seem plausible either to fast-talk the head nurse or to steal your mother's chart.''

''You amaze me.''

''I know that she lives in a world of her own, but I don't know how long she's been there, or why. What happened to her, Susannah?''

She gave the easy answer. ''The doctors don't know.''

''But you do, don't you?'' His voice was quiet.

''You think I drove her over the edge with the baby?''

''Come off it, Susannah. I think she went over that cliff all by herself—when the money was gone.''

Susannah closed her eyes and put her hand to her temple. Her voice was flat and so soft that he leaned closer in order to hear. ''You know that, too.''

''I didn't for a long time. Not till I saw your apartment and realized that you couldn't possibly have changed that much. You might not have wholeheartedly embraced your parents' way of life, but one thing you never lacked was style, Susannah. You wouldn't have chosen to live in a little square boxy apartment with odds and ends of furniture and dishes that don't match.''

''You think you know a lot, don't you, Marc?''

He looked at her for a long moment. ''I also know that the other thing you've never lacked is pride.''

Tears stung her eyelids. She turned her head away and tried to blink them back.

''So I looked up your parents in the newspaper files, and as soon as I found your father's obituary, I knew. He was very careful, wasn't he, so that it wouldn't look like suicide?''

Susannah knew he wasn't really asking a question, but she nodded anyway.

"I suppose it was then that your mother started on her long trip to nowhere?"

"She couldn't bear losing her position," Susannah said. "Her social standing, and her so-called friends. So she went off into a twilight world. And my father..." She swallowed hard. "He was stronger than she was, in a way—and yet he was weaker, too. He couldn't bear it any more than she could, but he couldn't follow her, either. So he brought it to an end."

"You must have sold everything they had," Marc said, "but it still wasn't enough. So you've impoverished yourself for years to keep her in that fancy home."

She leaped to contradict him. "It's not fancy, just extremely good. Care like that doesn't come cheap." For an instant, Susannah didn't realize how much of his speculation she'd admitted to. Then she saw the compassion in his eyes—or was it outright pity?—and anger flared within her. "Dammit, Marc, if you're quite finished pouring salt in the wound—"

"I did a pretty good job of it, didn't I?" He sounded almost rueful. "Tweaking you with being a snob...rubbing in your face that the Northbrook Millers..."

Susannah finished the sentence; it was easier to say it herself than to hear it spoken with sympathy. "—Were no longer anything at all."

"I wouldn't say that, exactly," Marc murmured. "There's one thing I still don't understand, Susannah. Why did you announce you were having a baby, in the first place?"

Part of her wanted to tell him, but the words seemed to stick in her throat. He sounded ready to listen—but if all she accomplished was to make him feel even more sorry for her... She fidgeted with the fringe on a sofa pillow so she couldn't be expected to look at him. "Why is it so important?"

"Don't you know?"

His voice was low, soft, like the rumble of distant thunder. Susannah felt herself start to tremble in a sort of sympathetic vibration. If her reasons mattered to him after all this time, could it mean *she* still mattered?

"I'd always wondered, you know," he mused. "It was such a foolish thing to say, if it wasn't fact—so surely it must have been the truth. And yet if there had been another man in your life, wouldn't I have known—or at least suspected? You weren't the sort to be playing with two men at a time."

"Thanks," Susannah muttered. "That's something, I suppose."

"Then when I saw you again, and there wasn't a child anywhere to be found... If there had been an accident to the pregnancy—a miscarriage or a stillbirth—why wouldn't you have admitted it? So perhaps, as strange as it sounded, there never was a child."

"You accused me of giving the baby up for adoption."

"Did I? I knew better, I think—if you'd borne a child, you'd have held on to it. I'd very nearly convinced myself of all that. And then I walked into your mother's room and heard you, calmly and matter-of-factly, saying you'd bring her granddaughter to visit, and the neat little tissue paper world I'd constructed exploded in my face. I'd built an image of you based on what I'd convinced myself you were. What I wanted you to be."

Susannah was afraid to breathe, afraid to move, for fear of shattering the incredible hope that was building inside her.

"And yet, so many things argued that you were still the woman I fell in love with all those years ago—and that you hadn't forgotten those days and those feelings, either. You even remembered that old dream of mine, of the ranch house in the suburbs, and even the sidewalk for kids to ride their bikes. If you recalled something like that in such vivid detail after so long, then surely you still felt something for me."

The words felt like warm oil against her skin—soothing, massaging, relieving pain so deep and so long-lived that she'd convinced herself it wasn't really pain at all.

"Then I found out about your mother's retreat from the world—and I understood that if she'd said she wanted to see little green men from Mars you'd have told her you'd bring half a dozen on your next trip. And then I knew what you'd meant when you said I hadn't listened."

She didn't realize he'd moved closer until she felt his warmth beside her and his breath stirring her hair.

"What would you have told me, Susannah, eight years ago—if I'd been wise enough to listen?"

She lifted her hands to her face in a gesture that was very like a prayer. "And if I'd been wise enough to understand," she said softly. "I don't think I did it deliberately, Marc—but I chose you to be a weapon against my parents."

He nodded. "I think I always knew that. You were so young, and so rebellious. I suppose that was why I was willing to believe the original story. What better way to destroy a pair of first-class snobs like your parents than by handing them an illegitimate grandchild? And you knew—you had to know—that I loved you so much I'd do almost anything for you."

"So of course you believed that I could use you like that."

"I'm sorry."

She shook her head. "No. It made sense—I can see that now. But that wasn't it at all, Marc. The pair of them tore into you like pit bulls, and I couldn't stand it. They were being so rude to you. So horribly, nastily, unnecessarily rude. They couldn't begin to see past the surface to the man underneath—the man I saw.''

He'd slid a little closer yet, and his arm closed around her, warm and supporting and comforting. She didn't want to ever have to move again.

''All you'd done to offend them was to say that you cared about me—but they were treating you as if it was a crime. I wanted it to stop, Marc. I wanted to show them how stupid and shallow they were. And suddenly, the words were just there—the one thing that was guaranteed to shake them up.''

''You did that, all right. And me, too.''

''I said it before I thought. As soon as the words were out, and I saw your face—I tried to tell you.''

''But I wouldn't listen. My outraged macho pride blinded me.''

''I never thought you'd take it seriously. And when you did...'' She swallowed hard. ''When I came to your room that day, I was going to throw myself on your mercy, try to explain, and hope that you'd understand. Then you told me you were leaving—without me.''

''I was offended at the idea that you'd led me on just to provide a handy scapegoat.'' His lips brushed her ear. ''And at the same time I couldn't help wishing it were all true, that you had cared enough about me to carry my child... Is it any wonder I had to get out of there before I could even start to think clearly?'' He tipped her face up to his and held her close, his forehead pressed against hers. ''So I left—and as soon as I'd walked away from you and it was too late to come back, I knew that I'd made the worst decision of my life. Susannah, there hasn't been a day in the last eight years I haven't wished that instead of blowing up because I felt my manhood threatened, I'd listened to my heart. I'd have put my arms around you and said biology doesn't matter, it's love that makes a family—and taken you with me, away from there..."

His arms were tight around her, and in the shelter of his body, Susannah knew she would always be safe. She raised her face to his.

Her ears were ringing when he stopped kissing her, and her breath rasped in her throat. "You're dangerous," she whispered, and settled close against his side. "Perhaps it's just as well," she said finally. "It wouldn't have worked, back then. You're right—I knew you worshiped me. I could have used you, taken advantage of you, in all kinds of ways. And I probably would have, stupid and immature as I was. You might have ended up hating me for it. But now..."

"Now is what counts, Susannah." His fingertips stroked her cheek and lifted her face to his, and she lost herself once more in the glory of loving him.

A good deal later, Marc said absently, "About Cyrus's pictures... Do you want to tell Pierce he can have the works, or shall I?"

Susannah pulled back from him just far enough to stare up into his eyes. "Honestly?"

"Of course—that's what Cyrus wanted, isn't it?"

"Yes—but I didn't think you believed that."

"Why wouldn't I? If you'd been faking it, you'd have done a much more convincing job."

"Thanks a lot." Indignant, she sat up straight.

Marc laughed and pulled her off balance and into his arms once more. "And the job at Universal Dynamics? Is Tryad interested in the contract?"

"I don't know," Susannah said doubtfully. "I'd have to be guaranteed the freedom to express myself."

"Where's the problem with that? You've already told Amos a thing or two."

"Amos is different."

"You mean you might hesitate to confront me?" His

tone was half teasing, half outraged. He pushed her gently back into the couch cushions and kissed her till Susannah was dizzy.

Finally she managed to say, "If that's how you plan to handle disagreements—"

"It's better than arguing, wouldn't you say? Shall we make it a tentative arrangement for a while? Put the contract on a trial basis and see how well we work together?"

Susannah considered, and a mischievous light crept into her eyes. "Okay. Only.... Marc, which of us is on probation?"

"Both," he said promptly. "But just so we understand each other, there's no trial period on the rest of the deal. This is for real, Susannah. And as for that business of you not sleeping with married men—"

"Oh, I suppose I could make an exception for you," she offered. "If you insist."

"That's good. Because I'm going to be very married. Soon—and forever."

"I can't argue with that," Susannah murmured, and then his kiss once more blotted out the world.

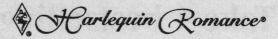

Harlequin Romance®

is delighted to bring you
a brilliant new trilogy
from bestselling author

Leigh
Michaels

Finding _Mr Right_

Three women definitely _not_ looking for
love—but it finds them anyway!

Kit, Susannah and Alison are best friends and partners.
Successful and happily single, they're busy running their own
business and have no intention of looking for husbands...
until each finds a man they simply can't resist!

Find your Mr Right, starting in March:

March 1998—THE BILLIONAIRE DATE (#3496)
April 1998—THE PLAYBOY ASSIGNMENT (#3500)
May 1998—THE HUSBAND PROJECT (#3504)

Available in March, April and May,
wherever Harlequin books are sold.

Take 4 bestselling love stories FREE

Plus get a FREE surprise gift!

This April
DEBBIE MACOMBER

takes readers to the Big Sky and beyond...

MONTANA

At her grandfather's request, Molly packs up her kids and returns to his ranch in Sweetgrass, Montana.

But when she arrives, she finds a stranger, Sam Dakota, working there. Molly has questions: What exactly is he doing there? Why doesn't the sheriff trust him? Just *who* is Sam Dakota? These questions become all the more critical when her grandfather tries to push them into marriage....

Moving to the state of Montana is one thing; entering the state of matrimony is quite another!

Available in April 1998 wherever books are sold.

MIRA

MDM434

Harlequin Romance®

Invites You to A Wedding!

Whirlwind Weddings
Combines the heady romance of a whirlwind courtship with the excitement of a wedding— strong heroes, feisty heroines and marriages made not so much in heaven as in a hurry!

What's the catch? All our heroes and heroines meet and marry within a week! Mission impossible? Well, a lot can happen in seven days....

January 1998—#3487 MARRY IN HASTE
by Heather Allison

February 1998—#3491 DASH TO THE ALTAR
by Ruth Jean Dale

March 1998—#3495 THE TWENTY-FOUR-HOUR BRIDE
by Day Leclaire

April 1998—#3499 MARRIED IN A MOMENT
by Jessica Steele

Who says you can't hurry love?

Available wherever Harlequin books are sold.

Catch more great

⬥ HARLEQUIN™ Movies

featured on the movie channel ⓜ

Premiering April 11th
Hard to Forget
based on the novel by bestselling
Harlequin Superromance® author
Evelyn A. Crowe

Don't miss next month's movie!
Premiering May 9th
The Awakening
starring Cynthia Geary and David Beecroft
based on the novel by Patricia Coughlin

If you are not currently a subscriber to
The Movie Channel, simply call your
local cable or satellite provider for more
details. Call today, and don't miss out
on the romance!

 **the movie channel ⓜ**   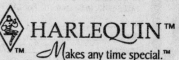 ⬥ **HARLEQUIN™**   *Makes any time special.*™

100% pure movies.
100% pure fun.

An Alliance Television Production

HARLEQUIN ULTIMATE GUIDES™

A series of how-to books for today's woman.

Act now to order some of these extremely
helpful guides just for you!

*Whatever the situation, Harlequin Ultimate Guides™
has all the answers!*

#80507	HOW TO TALK TO A	$4.99 U.S. ☐	
	NAKED MAN	$5.50 CAN. ☐	
#80508	I CAN FIX THAT	$5.99 U.S. ☐	
		$6.99 CAN. ☐	
#80510	WHAT YOUR TRAVEL AGENT	$5.99 U.S. ☐	
	KNOWS THAT YOU DON'T	$6.99 CAN. ☐	
#80511	RISING TO THE OCCASION		
	More Than Manners: Real Life	$5.99 U.S. ☐	
	Etiquette for Today's Woman	$6.99 CAN. ☐	
#80513	WHAT GREAT CHEFS	$5.99 U.S. ☐	
	KNOW THAT YOU DON'T	$6.99 CAN. ☐	
#80514	WHAT SAVVY INVESTORS	$5.99 U.S. ☐	
	KNOW THAT YOU DON'T	$6.99 CAN. ☐	
#80509	GET WHAT YOU WANT OUT OF	$5.99 U.S. ☐	
	LIFE—AND KEEP IT!	$6.99 CAN. ☐	

(quantities may be limited on some titles)

TOTAL AMOUNT	$
POSTAGE & HANDLING	$
($1.00 for one book, 50¢ for each additional)	
APPLICABLE TAXES*	$ _____
TOTAL PAYABLE	$ _____
(check or money order—please do not send cash)	

To order, complete this form and send it, along with a check or money
order for the total above, payable to Harlequin Ultimate Guides, to:
In the U.S.: 3010 Walden Avenue, P.O. Box 9047, Buffalo, NY
14269-9047; **In Canada:** P.O. Box 613, Fort Erie, Ontario, L2A 5X3.

Name: _____

Address: _____ City: _____

State/Prov.: _____ Zip/Postal Code: _____

*New York residents remit applicable sales taxes.
Canadian residents remit applicable GST and provincial taxes.

◆ HARLEQUIN®

Look us up on-line at: http://www.romance.net